Chapter 1

One a.m. on Christmas morning.

Remington Martinez's first white Christmas.

Texans in the panhandle probably saw the white stuff, but he was from southwest Texas. He'd spent the last two months on an Alaskan fishing boat, so this wasn't his first rodeo, but it was definitely his first white Christmas.

If Ford Hanson had his way, it'd be Rem's last Christmas as a single man.

He parked his three-quarter ton dually in front of the all-night gas station and walked inside. He didn't need fuel, but he needed to stretch his legs. Grab a joe maybe. Although from what he'd experienced so far, northerners didn't know how to make coffee. They seemed to use tweezers to measure the grounds instead of a spade shovel, the way coffee was meant to be made.

It wasn't the only thing northerners didn't get right, but it was his current gripe. That, and the cold.

His truck said -17. He'd never actually seen that little line in front of his truck's temperature display until yesterday coming down out of Canada, which was like coming down out of another world.

'Course he was back in the good ol' US of A, but he felt more like he'd moved into a Siberian village.

Maybe he looked like he was ready to spend the winter in Siberia. But the sleepy store clerk and the lady who walked in behind him carrying two children while a third trailed behind her weren't wearing a fur-lined parka, insulated coveralls, and one thousand-gram insulated hiking boots like he was. Actually, from his limited experience with the hardy North Dakotans, he was somewhat surprised the woman wasn't wearing flip-flops and a bikini.

The farther north he'd come, the odder folks had got.

The woman thanked him for holding the door for her and walked straight to the bathroom while he went to the coffee maker.

The stuff looked like weak tea, but Rome wasn't built in a day, and he wasn't going to teach the entire northern part of the country to make good coffee tonight, so he reached for a cup.

But he didn't pick it up because the little kid that had been trailing behind the woman passed the end of the aisle, heading toward the door.

Rem hesitated. He didn't usually get mixed up in other folk's business, but it was cowboy cold outside, and that little guy only had some kind of pajama thing on. Didn't even have real shoes, just little footie things connected to his pants.

He'd never spent much time with kids—he didn't allow his mind to go to the dark place where he remembered what his fiancée had done—and didn't know much of anything about them. But shouldn't he have a coat on at least?

The little guy pushed at the heavy door.

Rem's eyes went to the store clerk. He sat on the stool by the register, his arms crossed over his chest, his head back, eyes closed, mouth open, snoring.

Figures.

Rem glanced over at the bathroom. The door was closed.

He adjusted his hat and leaned down, looking out the window. A car with the parking lights on sat at a gas pump, like the woman might have fueled up before walking in. There wasn't anyone in the passenger seat.

A set of headlights flashed from a car just pulling into the parking lot.

Rem couldn't let the little guy go outside by himself with who knows what kind of stranger out there.

The kid hadn't gotten the door open yet.

Just when Rem decided he might not have to worry about it because the kid couldn't get out, the kid gave a huge shove, and the door popped open.

Rem swore.

He took two long steps over to the kid, grabbed him by the seat of his pants, and swung him up under his arm. He didn't exactly know how one was supposed to carry a kid that size, smaller than a newborn calf but bigger than his cattle dog.

The kid started screaming like he'd put a firecracker in his pants, so it probably wasn't the way he was used to being carried.

Rem strode over to the bathroom, hoping to set the screaming thing down in front of the door, and hopefully his mother would be out before he could make it to the outside door again.

He should have known from all the years he'd worked with animals. One didn't castrate a piglet within hearing distance of its mother. He'd seen nine hundred-pound sows climb a five-foot fence to get to their precious, squealing porkers. A sight like that helped a man find a way to drop the piglet and climb the nearest cottonwood.

But that angry sow didn't have a thing on the human mamma that came barreling out of that restroom, a baby in each arm, and he wouldn't have been surprised to see a gun in her teeth, pointed at his privates with the trigger half squeezed.

A blast of cold air rocked the store as the outside door opened, but Rem didn't take his eyes off the hollering woman in front of him. He closed his mouth over the explanation he'd been ready to give, dropped the kid, raised his hands in the air—despite her lack of a visible gun—and backed slowly away. He knew when he was outmatched.

The woman ducked forward and grabbed her offspring with one of the hands that still held a baby.

She glanced over at the door. "Watch this guy. He just tried to take my boy. Probably a child trafficker or molester or something. He's obviously not from around these parts."

How did she know he wasn't from around these parts? Did he have it stamped on his forehead? He resisted the urge to touch his forehead under his hat brim and kept his hands in the air.

She didn't have the smooth southern tones of women he was used to hearing, but he hadn't gotten a word out of his mouth, so she wouldn't know he didn't have the clipped and jarring sound of a Yankee.

"Thanks for the warning. I left my other kids in the car with the motor running." A voice, smooth as saddle leather and just a bit husky, came from his left, and he turned toward it, wondering at the stirring deep in the pit of his stomach.

A frail-looking woman, with hair as fair as his was black, wearing a long black skirt and a sparkling red top, like she'd just come from church, stood holding onto the hand of a boy not much bigger than the one he'd just tried to keep from walking outside and freezing to death. Not like anyone around here appreciated it.

"I'll watch it for you, sister." The woman who'd just come out of the bathroom huffed.

"Thanks, I'll just be a minute." The frail woman, with wrists maybe only twice as big around as his thumb, gave him a suspicious look before tugging on the hand of her child and keeping an eye on him as she walked to the bathroom. He kept his hands in the air, but his eyes tracked her as she moved. Her eyes were tired, her face careworn, but her movements were graceful and confident.

Still, she walked by him like he was a rat sticking its nose out of a hole.

He'd never felt so much like a criminal in his life before.

Apparently they put antifreeze in their veins come winter up here, since the red shirt that lady was wearing was short sleeved. Obviously the other kid hadn't needed saving, either. Maybe his sleeper was made of heat tape.

At this point in time, he just wanted to get the tinted water these folks called coffee and finish the drive to his friend Ford's home, where he'd stay for Christmas before getting directions to the home of his future wife. She apparently had four wild children, a dog that learned its manners north of the Mason-Dixon line, and a dilapidated home that was slightly more crooked than a DC politician. But she had a ranch and, as soon as she married him, a billion dollars. That was his paraphrase of Ford's description.

Ford hadn't actually told him what the woman herself looked like.

The bathroom door clicked, and the white-blond woman in the sparkling red shirt walked out holding tight to the hand of her little boy. Her eyes scanned the store until her gaze hooked on his.

He expected to see a return of the suspicion and disdain on her face. But like the time in the restroom had given her a minute to think things through, those emotions didn't appear. Instead, her gaze was wary but thoughtful, too.

Rem had been a professional bull rider for over a decade. He thrived on the excitement and challenge. But he'd also learned to pay attention to the subtle signs.

He wasn't in any danger of being attacked by this woman. For some reason, he wanted to defend himself, even though she wasn't even the woman whose kid he'd saved.

But he'd learned, too, that a woman who looked soft and sweet could hurt him worse than a one-ton bull.

Actually, if he had to choose between his ex-fiancée, who was now his sister-in-law, and the one-ton bull…he'd take the bull, easy choice.

This woman's ice-blue eyes, the color of which reminded him of the Texas sky at high noon, warmed him. Without thinking, the manners of his childhood kicked in.

He tipped his hat and said, "Merry Christmas, ma'am."

It was almost imperceptible, but she slowed just a bit, and her brows twitched. Then she jerked her chin up, acknowledging his words, and walked out the door.

~~~

"Mommy, Mommy, open this."

"I need batteries."

"Wook at me, Mommy. Wook at me."

"Can I get this out now?"

Elaine's head throbbed, and like pretty much every day for the last two years, she felt like crying. She'd gotten so used to not letting the tears fall—not in front of the children at least—that her eyes didn't prick, and she didn't give it conscious thought.

Instead, she sat at the kitchen table, cognizant it was Christmas Day, and smiled at her three-year-old who wanted her to watch him, while correcting her older children. "When you ask, you need to say please."

Did they have batteries? She wasn't sure.

Why did they make the toy containers so difficult to open, anyway? Did stores really have a shoplifting problem with three-year-olds?

Maybe they just wanted to punish parents for having children.

Elaine truly appreciated her neighbors to the east, Ford and Morgan, Ty and Louise, Palmer and Ames, for inviting them in yesterday and giving her children gifts that she couldn't afford. It had been kind and thoughtful and made Christmas sweet for her kids, since she was hardly going to her own family's celebration.

But the chaos around her never stopped. With a glance at her phone, she realized it would be time to go feed soon. She was already bone-weary. Maybe, since it was Christmas, she'd let the kids settle down in front of the TV for a while this evening.

Just as she finished opening the package and handed it over to her three-year-old's mumbled "thank you," her phone rang.

It was her mother's number, and she almost didn't answer it.

But it was Christmas.

"Hello?" she said, trying not to sound as tired as she felt.

"Are you coming?" Her mother's tone wasn't unkind, but there was a trace of annoyance in her voice, like she was catering to Elaine.

"I told you three weeks ago I wasn't." She could not make the drive to Fargo without having someone feed the stock for her. That, however, was the least of her issues.

"I don't know why you're holding a grudge about this. You're keeping your children away from your family and punishing them over your inability to get past your issues." Her mother sounded wheedling and exasperated by turns.

"I told you that you were welcome to come here."

"But James and Corrie wouldn't have anywhere to go. Unless you've decided to forgive and move on?"

Was there really something wrong with her because she still had a hang-up with her husband running off with her sister? Was it that unreasonable of her to not want to ruin her Christmas by seeing them and their new baby? She'd also have to deal with all the questions of her own kids—why Daddy didn't come see them, why he didn't live here anymore, and, from her older ones, what had she done to make him hate them.

She was bone-tired, about to lose the ranch, and worried how she was going to support four children on her own once she did. Was it really that selfish of her to not want to have to face her cheating ex-husband and her little sister?

The betrayal of her sister hurt worse than the cheating of her husband. They were exactly twelve months apart, sharing the same birthdate in January.

But it couldn't be good for her children for their mother to be holding a grudge against their father, no matter how badly she'd been treated. She needed to get over it. It was best for the children, and best for her mental health, too.

At that moment, an image from last night, or in reality, early this morning, cut through her brain. A man, tall and dark with flashing black eyes and a drawl as big as the North Dakota sky, came to mind. She shook the image off, even though she didn't believe that he'd actually been trying to take that little boy. What he had been doing, though, she couldn't say.

"Maybe next year, Mom. I told you I can't drive the whole way to Fargo and still get the stock fed."

"And I could see right through that for the excuse it is. I understand what James did was wrong, but you're punishing the entire family by your stubborn refusal to set your differences aside for just a little while at Christmas." Her mother sounded so hurt and disappointed.

Elaine had never wanted to hurt anyone, and she hated disappointing her mother.

"It's too late this year." Who knew how things were going to play out. Unless a miracle happened, she wouldn't have the ranch next year. It was all she'd known all her life. She had no idea what she'd do when the bank took it.

"Too late for Christmas, but I'm going to plan a big birthday celebration for you and Corrie next month. I expect you to be here."

"I can't, Mom. You know I can't leave the stock." It was an excuse, a great one, since this time of year, she really couldn't leave.

"Then we'll have it at your house. Unless you want to keep nursing your bruised feelings and jealousy over your sister's happiness."

For the first time in her conversation with her mother, heat crawled up the back of Elaine's neck, and pressure built in her ~~neck~~temples. She gritted her teeth.

"I am not jealous." That was the honest truth. She didn't want happiness if it involved James. Their divorce terms had dictated that he didn't have to pay child support, but in return, he signed away his parental rights. That was the only happiness she had wanted from James.

"Then stop acting like it," her mother said, sounding a bit harsh in her firmness.

Elaine couldn't blame her. Not much. She'd want her children to get along, too. But when she talked to her mother, her mother always made it seem like everything was her fault.

"We'll have the party at your house, the last Saturday in January." Her mother's words sounded like nails being driven into her coffin.

Elaine couldn't decline without a big fight. That much was obvious. She swallowed her anger and hurt. "That's fine, Mom. Next month, a party at my house."

Chapter 2

Remington followed Ford and Morgan down the windswept driveway of what could be his future home if things went the way Ford expected them to.

Rem didn't mind the isolation. Where he'd lived in west Texas, things were just as isolated. And after the years he'd spent as one of the top professional bull riders in the country, with hordes of people following after him, mostly women if he were being honest, peace and quiet was something he valued.

Sure looked like there'd be peace and quiet here. At least from the nonexistent neighbors. The black lab that bounded out on the porch was everything Ford had warned him about. He allowed a grin to tug up the corners of his mouth as the dog jumped on Ford who set a well-placed knee to its chest, knocking the big thing over.

It bounded back up, tail going like the Texas wind, and sidled up to Ford—keeping all four paws on the ground.

Rem parked his dually beside Ford's SUV and got out as Ford opened Morgan's door. Rem still got a good chuckle out of Ford's deformed face and figure next to Morgan's exquisite loveliness. They weren't a match that anyone would have predicted, but they were perfect for each other and obviously in love.

Love hadn't worked out so well for Rem. It'd almost be easier if he had deformities. He didn't have to worry about women wanting his money, since he'd sunk most of the cash he'd earned as a bull rider into his father's ranch, thinking it would be his one day.

Then he and his dad had fought, about something stupid – how fast to expand their herd – but the fight had quickly escalated, not helped by his younger brother, Maximus, and his dad decided to cut him out of his will, planning to give everything to Max. Funny, but that's when Olivia had decided she'd actually wanted to marry Max.

At that point, it had almost been a relief to Rem, since he'd never gotten over what Olivia had done with his money.

The dog bounded over. A perfectly timed elbow kept him in line, and Rem patted the top of his slobbering head.

By this time, three small, white-haired children had lined the porch. The figure of their mother stood in the doorway, partially in shadow as she held the youngest.

Rem walked around, grabbing the last of the groceries—a box of bulk hamburger—that Ford had brought.

Ford had given him the lowdown on this woman, her story and a few facts about the kids and ranch.

None of it really mattered to Rem, though. She had a ranch, a good spread that could be profitable with the right oversight and management, and she had an inheritance of one billion dollars that would be theirs when they married.

If he married this woman, took her kids as his own, he'd have everything he'd lost in Texas. Except decent weather. He'd only been in North Dakota for two days, but he'd take Texas hot and dry over North Dakota cold and snow any day of the week.

The ramshackle house looked like a sapling in a windstorm. It leaned toward the south, so Rem walked up the north side of the steps, just to try to balance things out.

He wasn't afraid of marriage. Nor of kids. Nor of hard work, which is what this place needed, and a lot of it. Actually there wasn't much he was afraid of.

He had a healthy respect for the bulls he rode, and to say he'd never been scared would be a big, fat lie. He was scared every time he got on. It was part of the high, part of the draw—to face that fear and win.

Scared, yes. Afraid? No way.

So, the tingle in his stomach felt familiar. It made him smile. A cocky grin, maybe. Because, oh yeah—he looked at the kids and the dog, the listing of the porch—this would be a challenge.

The house shook as the dog bounded up the stairs.

More than a challenge.

But he wasn't afraid, and he'd never backed down from a challenge. He could do this. Turning this ranch into a profitable grass-fed beef operation would take money, time, and a lot of hard work, but excitement shivered in his chest. He'd enjoy conquering these challenges.

He'd have to marry a stranger, but after his experience with Olivia, it couldn't be any worse. Actually, the idea of being unconventional, flaunting what society expected, choosing his own path, and marching down it was very appealing.

People thought he was crazy because he rode bulls. Maybe he was. Maybe this proved it. Because seeing this place had only confirmed what he already knew—the challenge the whole situation presented excited him on an elemental level, and he couldn't wait to get started.

He reached the top step behind Ford and Morgan, the box of groceries in his hands. He hadn't even seen the woman who could become his wife. Morgan had insisted she was pretty. Ford had said maybe she would be if she weren't so worn out. He didn't even care.

A flash from last night—blond hair, Texas-sky eyes, and a voice like warm honey—shot through his memory, but he pushed it aside. He'd lived long enough to know that women were never what they seemed, and he was tired of playing the game.

"Hi, Elaine," Morgan said. "I hope you all had a nice Christmas."

The woman adjusted the baby and nodded. The kids all bounded around, laughing and talking. They seemed familiar and at ease with Ford and Morgan. They'd kept their distance from him, but he wasn't great with kids, so it wasn't surprising. He'd work on that in his spare time.

The porch shook as the dog thumped around. It needed to be replaced, no doubt. Maybe the whole house did. He'd have to do a closer inspection if the lady decided to go through with it.

The idea that she wouldn't was a distinct possibility. Ford and Morgan had said that her children were her first priority and she wouldn't do anything that might put them in danger. Which is why she hadn't advertised for a husband. He could respect that. It actually put this woman, Elaine, in a different category than Olivia.

"I know we're a little early, but if you don't mind starting ten minutes before we planned, we'd like to come in and introduce you two and chat for a while." Morgan had a smile in her voice.

"My bread isn't quite ready, but come on in. We can talk until it is."

The voice sent shivers down his spine. Rem's eyes widened. Those honeyed tones sounded the same as the lady from last night. In front of him, Ford shifted at the same time the realization struck Rem, and he saw the woman in the doorway clearly for the first time.

Hair so blond it was almost white. Lines of fatigue around her face and eyes. A slender body and delicate bone structure that flew in the face of the harsh North Dakota wind and the grinding poverty around them. And those eyes. Like the Texas sky at high noon. Yeah, they were looking at him and definitely saying shoot-out. Only he'd left his handgun in the pickup. It wasn't a revolver, and he didn't have a side holster, but from the look on her face, he wasn't sure it mattered.

She recognized him, all right. Her arms tightened around her baby. She stepped back, but her eyes were narrowed, and they stuck on him like stink on a hog.

He tipped his hat at her. "Ma'am," he said as he walked by. Three little bodies raced by before the door thumped closed like the gate in a starting pen. It was going to take a little more time to get this figured out, and he'd have to hold on a lot longer than an eight-second ride.

He eyed the kids. He couldn't all the sudden pretend he was great with kids and they loved him. That would be the best option right now, but he wouldn't be fooling anyone, least of all the woman who'd just made a wide berth around him and indicated the table where they could all sit.

He followed Ford and Morgan as they set their boxes on the counter.

"Gabriel," Elaine said, "you and Heaven can start that movie like I told you we'd do when our guests came."

"Yes, ma'am," the tallest of the kids said before he and the little girl with long pigtails took the other little ones into the next room.

The woman's eyes landed on his shoulder before she smiled at Ford and Morgan. "Please sit."

The kitchen smelled like baking bread and apples with cinnamon. He could walk into a kitchen that smelled like this every day.

He pulled out a chair. The thing wobbled and didn't look any sturdier than the metal and Formica table. He lowered himself carefully on one side of the table, noting that Ford did the same, sitting beside Morgan on the other side.

Both ends and the chair beside him were available as Elaine opened the oven door and looked inside.

"The bread will be ready in ten minutes." She shut the oven door and cleared her throat. "I can get everyone some water."

"Yes, please," Morgan said.

"I'll take a glass, too," Ford said.

Rem stood. He wasn't used to being waited on and didn't intend to get soft even if he did get married.

The woman had her back to him. She wore a t-shirt and jeans and looked just as thin as she had in the gas station. When Ford had said she'd had four kids, Rem had kind of pictured a matronly woman, maybe a little older than himself, with lots of curves and some padding to go with them. Not the skeletal child in front of him. He'd been thinking they'd be working side by side, but she didn't look like she could carry a gallon of tea to the table, let alone do any kind of ranch work.

He opened the freezer door. As he suspected, there was a tray of ice right in front, and he pulled it out.

"Grab one for me, too," he said as the woman pulled three glasses out of the cupboard. One hinge held the crooked door on.

"You can say 'please,'" the honeyed voice chided him as her hand brought down a fourth glass.

"Thank you," he said. No point in letting her think he was some pansy-waisted pudding dumpling that would do whatever she said.

He shut the freezer and twisted the tray. As he was debating about washing his hands, she set a pair of tongs on the counter without looking at him. He picked them up and set two cubes in each glass, noticing that her eyes lingered on his hands. They were big and brown next to her delicate white ones.

He couldn't do anything about his size nor the color of his skin. Nor how the sun had darkened it even more, and nothing about what lay under his clothes. If she had a problem with any of it, when they sat down at the table, she'd better speak up.

Pretty sure it wasn't going to matter. Ford or Morgan would have known if it was an issue. But why else would she be staring at his hands?

Stepping around her, he filled up the empty spots in the tray with water from the tap and walked it back to the freezer. By that time, she had two glasses filled with water, and he grabbed them, setting them in front of Ford and Morgan.

Elaine came behind him with the other two. She met his eyes, briefly, before she set one down in front of the chair where his hat hung. In a deliberate decision, she set the other one down in front of the chair beside it.

A shot of victory surged through him, like it might when the gate opened and the bull surged out. There were times he just knew, right at that moment, that he'd be riding through the horn.

When she set the glass down at the seat beside him, that's the moment he knew that the frail woman with four kids, a ten thousand-acre ranch, and a billion-dollar inheritance would be standing with him in front of a preacher.

Chapter 3

Elaine pulled her chair out with hands that trembled. She did not give voice to the sigh that pressed against her lips. The man's presence seemed to fill up her kitchen, but she had to say he'd impressed her when he'd gotten up and helped with the drinks. He wasn't a man to sit around and wait for things to come to him. She liked that. He wasn't afraid, wasn't bashful, and wasn't going to tiptoe around, worried about stepping on toes or making a mistake.

She appreciated his confident carriage. The sure way he moved, almost graceful. She liked the lack of guile in his eyes, as well. He was here for the ranch and the money. He knew the kids and she came with it, and he wasn't making bones about the fact that he wouldn't be interested in her or her children if it weren't for the ranch and money. Maybe that should bother her, but it actually gave her a good feeling. He wasn't pretending to be something he was not just to get what he wanted.

Ford looked at them across the table. "Morgan and I aren't going to stay. But I just wanted to make sure that you knew, Elaine, that I had my lawyer look into Rem, with his permission. The lawyer had a full and comprehensive background check done plus did interviews with Rem's friends and family. He documented everything he found, including the time he threw a tissue out of his truck window when he was nineteen."

Rem snorted.

If Elaine hadn't been so nervous, she might have smiled.

Morgan pulled a binder out of the shoulder bag she'd set on the floor. Ford pushed it across the table.

"Rem did not go through it. He said he's not hiding anything. With his permission, this is the full report from my lawyer."

Elaine desperately wanted a drink to get rid of the lump in her dry throat, but she reached for the folder instead.

"My lawyer went through his background as carefully as possible. Morgan and I both read every word. Rem has no criminal record other than the two times he was arrested back in his early twenties."

Elaine's head popped up. He'd been arrested?

"I was drunk both times," Rem said in that slow southern drawl that made tingles prance up her spine. "I quit drinking after the second time. I wanted a championship worse than I wanted liquor." He jerked his head at the binder. "Maybe that's in there, too."

"It is," Ford confirmed.

Elaine wondered if he wasn't going after a "championship" anymore, would he still not drink. She'd not read the report yet, of course, but it sounded like he'd had a drinking problem at some point.

"You two are going to work this out among yourselves. I just wanted to ease your mind, Elaine. We've checked and vetted him the best we can. I've done business with him for years.

He has my highest recommendation, otherwise I wouldn't be here." Ford's blue eye was sincere as he looked across the table at her. "We did answer some of his questions, too, but of course we didn't do a background check on you. Morgan saw your letter, and we know it's legit, so the money that he's looking for is actually available. Also, we went to the courthouse and did a title search on your deed. He knows how much you owe."

Elaine had not really believed they would find someone who was willing to take on a wife and four small children when she'd given Morgan permission to look her up.

Morgan glanced at the men then spoke. "We don't want to get between you two. Whatever you work out is up to you. But we wanted to make sure you're comfortable before we leave."

Under the table, Elaine's knees shook so bad they almost knocked together, but she curled her lips up, hoping she didn't look as scared as she felt.

"I really appreciate all that you two have done for me. I know Mr. Martinez must be a little crazy to agree to this in the first place."

The man beside her snorted and drained his glass of water.

"But I also know that you two care about me and my children and would never let anything happen if it were in your power to prevent it. Thank you."

"You're very welcome." Morgan got up and walked around the table, waiting for Elaine to stand before giving her a big hug.

Ford stood, shaking Rem's hand.

Elaine walked to the oven. "The bread is ready. You two can stay and have some."

"If you're okay, we're going to head home. I have some business to take care of." Ford's eye patch made him look like a benevolent pirate. Morgan stopped at his side, slipping her arm around his waist. Her height matched him perfectly, but it was the way she looked at him—a look he returned—that told better than anything that they were perfect together.

Ford and Rem seemed to communicate without words for a brief moment before Ford opened the door and he and Morgan walked out.

Elaine didn't look at Rem but turned to the stove and pulled the bread out. Her children were being good, thankfully. They weren't usually allowed to watch TV in the middle of the day, so typically, it kept them entertained as long as it was on. Hopefully Rem and she would be done with everything they needed to discuss before the movie was over.

She set plates, butter, jelly, and knives on the table before slicing the bread and setting it down as well.

Rem had sat back down, and he watched her. She could feel his eyes on her back. Those black eyes in his dark face with the straight black hair that was just slightly longer than she'd choose to allow it to be.

She willed her hands not to tremble as she turned and pulled her chair back out. "I guess this is where I ask you what was going on Christmas night when we met in the gas station."

His half-grin was lazy and almost arrogant. "I think you already figured out that I didn't do what that woman was accusing me of."

She'd known that before she'd left the restroom with Elijah. Rem was big and strong, and if he'd wanted to leave the store with her kid, that woman wasn't going to stop him, especially since she was already holding two children. The clerk didn't seem overly concerned, either.

"Maybe." She nodded at the bread. "You can eat while you talk."

His eyes crinkled, but he didn't say anything as he picked up a slice of bread and a knife. As they had a little bit ago, his hands fascinated her. Long and strong, his fingers were brown and rough with more than an average amount of white scars on them. It wasn't hard to picture those hands fixing fences or forking hay. Driving a tractor or moving cattle. It was a little harder to picture them holding her children. Or touching her.

She shivered and looked away.

"The kid was going to walk outside. She was busy in the restroom with the other two. I thought it was too cold for a little guy like that to be out by himself, so when he opened the door, I picked him up, tucked him under my arm, and planned to deposit him back in front of the bathroom door."

Ah, it all made sense now. "I saw you pick him up and walk toward the bathroom. If you'd been trying to take him, it would have been easy for you to walk out the door."

"Yeah, well, I hadn't counted on him being quite so loud."

She tapped her chin. "Kids are loud."

His eyes slanted toward the room where her kids were watching TV. "Yours are being quiet."

Busted. "I don't typically allow them to watch TV, but I thought it was important that we talk uninterrupted, and I knew that was the one sure way."

"I see." He finished spreading the jelly on his bread and took a bite, the bread still steaming.

His jaw worked up and down about three times before his brows raised and his eyes flashed to her.

He swallowed before saying, "Good stuff."

Her lips twitched, and her chest felt a hundred times lighter. She wasn't the best cook in the world; there were a lot of things she didn't do well. But she made great bread, rolls, sweet rolls, and anything that took yeast. James hadn't cared for her baking abilities.

She had a tendency to bake when she was nervous—hence the bread today. It relaxed her and also reminded her that there were things in life she could control. Things she was good at.

"Thanks," she said.

He took another bite and chewed, seemingly completely comfortable with the silence that stretched between them and in no hurry to get to any kind of important discussion. A stark contrast to James's tightly wound nervousness and constant motion.

She should quit comparing the two. The situations were completely different. She had thought she was in love with James. She didn't have any such illusions about Rem. James and she had hopes and dreams and the naivety of youth. Rem wasn't a young kid any longer, and neither was she. She felt a lot older than her twenty-seven years, and she had a hunch that bull riding probably aged a man pretty fast, too.

Using her thumbnail, she picked at the edge of the plate. There were a million unformed questions and issues in her head that she knew they needed to discuss. But whether it was his nearness, or his commanding nature, or maybe just the reality of the situation had settled in, she couldn't think of a thing.

Rem had finished the piece of bread he'd been eating and picked up another. "I spent the last two months on an Alaskan fishing boat. Hard work and I loved the challenge, but the food sucked. This is good."

Her heart dropped a little more. ~~when he said where he'd been.~~ She didn't want a man who jumped from challenge to challenge and couldn't stay in one spot. Like James. He'd gotten tired of Elaine, so he'd told her he had a job on Friday nights. Instead he'd been taking Corrie out and romancing her.

Yeah. She needed to stop comparing the two men, but hearing that Rem loved a challenge was a big red flag for her.

"I suppose it was challenging to be a bull rider as well?" she said, hoping it was a casual and natural continuation of the conversation. She was a bit out of practice at conversing with adults.

"Yeah." His teeth flashed white in his face, and his eyes shone. "Life is a challenge, and I like to hit it head-on." He spread his hands out. "This is a challenge, and I know I'm up for it."

Elaine tried to boost her sagging spirits. She knew she would never get a play-it-safe kind of guy to take on what she was offering. She needed a man like Rem. If only he didn't constantly remind her of James. She hadn't been enough to keep James here and happy. After two years, she'd mostly come to terms with the fact that it hadn't been her responsibility to make him honor his vows, but she still had that part of her that whispered there was something wrong with her because her husband wouldn't stay true.

"I'm glad."

"You don't sound it." His eyes had narrowed some, and he was studying her.

"You're right. It's going to be a challenge. I guess I just don't want you to 'meet' this challenge then go looking for the next challenge in your life." She lifted a shoulder, unable to look at him. "Or maybe you'll get tired of the kids. It gets crazy in here. Or maybe you'll get tired of the cold and the snow, the isolation, the darkness, the mess, the chaos. Or…maybe you'll get tired of me." Her voice wasn't as strong at the end as she wanted it to be.

She could handle anything. He could snore. Throw his clothes on the floor. Leave the toothpaste lid off. Squeeze from the middle. Put the toilet paper roll on so it hung over instead of under—holy smokes, she'd just love to have someone else actually replace an empty roll of toilet paper!

With a billion dollars, he could even waste money and she would bite her lips hard to keep from complaining about that. But she couldn't stand another man who left.

"I assumed we'd be married in front of a preacher," he said slowly.

Her brows knitted together. "I thought so too."

"If I say I'm staying, especially in front of a preacher with the Good Book open, I'm gonna die beside you, girl." His eyes were black as night and dead serious.

Somehow, she didn't doubt him for a second. "As long as you don't hurt my kids, that's all I need to know."

One side of his mouth kicked up, and he reached for another piece of bread. "I think that's what the binder's for. I've not been around kids much, but I don't have much of a temper. In my opinion, that's probably most of the problem with people that hurt kids." His eyes gazed out the window, where dusk had fallen. "That, and a whole lot of selfishness."

His voice was distant, and his gaze far away, like he might have been remembering something. Maybe from his own childhood? A previous girlfriend?

She was very curious, but if this were just a business transaction, then they didn't need to share personal stories any more than it took for them to be comfortable with the decision to get married. She closed her mouth over the questions she wanted to ask.

Folding her hands carefully together, she said, "Well then, is there anything you need to know about me or the ranch in order to help make your decision?"

He finished chewing before he answered. "I've made it."

Her mouth opened. "That's it? You don't need to think about it or ask anything or…anything?" she finished, feeling lame. How could he be so sure?

"No."

Her mouth flapped up and down like a fish out of water, but she just couldn't help it.

He reached for another slice of bread and must have taken pity on her because he spoke. "I assume you're not gonna get offended over this because you're the one looking for a husband, but you've got a nice spread here. Enough acreage to run several thousand head of beef, unless we want to branch out. Barn's in better shape than the house. You have a good well, and I think I saw three boys." He jerked his head at the room where her children were. "Ranch hands in ten years."

He looked down at the knife he held in his hand. "I'm not gonna starve. Just learned that today, and you're not bad to look at." He lifted his head and gave her a direct gaze. "But I'm not gonna lie to you. A billion dollars is a lot of money, and I'd marry an ex-con who went to prison for murdering her first husband with a toothpick and a butter knife in order to get it. Especially if she came with a spread this size." His black eyes sparked. "But I'd be sleeping with my handgun under my pillow."

She was grateful that he looked back down and spread butter over his bread, because as much as she didn't want to admit it, his words had hurt.

He was right. It was a business proposition that she had initiated. She would have bet money, if she had any, that every single shred of her feminine vanity had been shattered when James walked out on her.

She'd have lost money she didn't have. She might not know this guy, and she definitely wasn't in love with him, but her heart hurt.

No woman wanted to be told that they were second to money and a ranch. Of course her pride was wounded. She tried to tell herself that was all it was.

He finished spreading the butter and scooped some jelly out. He only had three more pieces, and he'd have eaten that whole loaf himself.

He planted his forearms on the table, holding the bread and knife still. "So, how about this? Ask me anything you want today. You read that report tonight. Then I'll come back tomorrow morning and help you feed. Once we're done with that and anything else that can't wait, ask me anything else you want. And if you're not comfortable then, we can do it for as many days as you need until you've eased your mind. I can see how a billion dollars and the ranch might not be worth it to have to put up with me hanging around for the rest of your life."

Her eyes flew to his after his last statement. She wasn't thinking like that at all. Maybe her lack of commitment was hurting him as much as his eagerness for the money had hurt her.

She spread her hands out. "It's nothing personal against you. If it were just me, you could have brought the preacher with you today, and we'd be married by now. You seem like a decent guy. Ford recommends you, which means a lot to me, and I think we could be friends." Her breath pushed out in a heavy sigh, and she fingered the edge of her plate. Her knees had quit trying to knock each other out, but her stomach hadn't settled enough that she was going to try to eat anything. "But it's not just me. I have to protect my children. I do have fears of my own, of course." A lot of them. "But I know I can handle whatever happens. I just don't want to put my children through anything more. An abuser. A man who's here, saying he's going to stay, then leaves. A drunk."

Rem flinched at that, and Elaine felt a little bad for hitting him where she knew he was vulnerable, but in her opinion, he needed to know where she stood.

He put his bread down and faced her in his chair. "That was fair. You'll see in that report that I *was* a drunk. It's documented. It took me twice, but I learned the lessons I needed to. I can promise you I don't touch alcohol."

Normally she wouldn't push. But she was going to marry this man. "What if something happens? Something really bad? Is getting drunk how you cope?"

He swallowed and looked away. Seconds ticked by. Finally he looked at the room where the small children were with a sliding glance then back at Elaine. His jaw jutted out. "Bad things? They've happened."

He stood. "Through them all, I didn't touch a drop of alcohol." He shoved his hat on his head.

Elaine's chest was balled so tight and hot she could barely breathe.

Rem put his hand on the door and stood there with his head down, looking at the floor. "You still thinking about taking me?"

"Yes."

"I'm gonna walk around outside for a bit. Thanks for the bread."

Elaine forced her mouth to work. "I'll be out in an hour to feed. If you're still around, you can help and stay for supper."

"I'll help you feed." He opened the door and walked out.

Chapter 4

Rem strode over the well-worn path through the snow. He'd thought this was going to be a business decision, never suspecting that he'd be tempted to share the details of the worst time of his life. Being tossed in jail didn't even begin to compare. He'd deserved that.

He walked around the barn. Saw a dilapidated building that must be a chicken coop. Checked out the small herd of Angus in the field closest to the barn. Noted the flimsy fence. In some places, it was fixed with binder twine.

Two tractors were parked in the bottom of the barn, and there were three horses in stalls. Two of them looked like decent grade horses. One looked like a high-dollar quarter horse that had passed his prime about fifteen years ago. His hip bones jutted out, and his neck seemed too skinny to hold his head, but he had the scars and the brand that bespoke the life of a working horse.

"Bet you were something, back in the day," he said as the old boy reached his head over his stall. The boards were fixed haphazardly and would never hold any horse that wanted out. But this guy was well-trained, and although a little of the fire from his youth still blazed in his eyes, there was wisdom and patience there, as well. He probably had enough zip in him to make her kids feel like real cowboys, while not so much that Elaine would worry about them getting hurt.

He scratched the big blaze on the wide, old forehead. "You're still doing a job. Still needed. Even if it's different than what you started out with."

He supposed the horse was like him. He missed the bull riding some. The attention and accolades. The respect. Up here, he'd yet to meet anyone who even recognized him. At least in Texas, he still garnered a hat tip and a back slap, if not full-out questions or even a request for his autograph. There, a championship bull rider was a big thing. They knew it wasn't easy.

Hadn't been easy on his body, either. He probably had just as many aches and pains as that old horse. His ankle and wrist ached no matter what the weather. His leg with the pin in it hurt like heck when they were going to get a storm.

His skull had a plate over it in the back—the injury that finally ended his career—but his hat and hair covered the scar most of the time.

His right shoulder had been dislocated more times than he could count. And he couldn't even say how many ribs he'd busted. No point in going to the doc for that. He could ride as soon as he could grit his teeth through the pain and not pass out.

Were those things he should disclose to Elaine? There was no such thing as a pain-free day for him, and he couldn't imagine it would get better with time.

The concussions might be the thing that she really ought to be told about.

His hand had stilled, and the old horse nuzzled his chest. "No treats, sorry, bud."

He scratched the ears, deciding that he wouldn't tell Elaine about his injuries. Maybe they'd be documented to some extent in the report anyway. From what Ford had said, Rem was her last hope. And from what she said, her only concern was her children. It wouldn't matter to her if he were too stoved up to work in a couple of years or so. With the kind of money she was going to get, she could hire people to work the ranch and wouldn't need him anyway.

He didn't like that thought.

Maybe trying to find a life after the accolades and excitement of being a champion bull rider was harder than he'd thought it would be. Of course, he'd thought he'd be joining his dad on their spread and breeding champion bucking bulls and horses. Hadn't thought he'd end up in the frozen north, in the middle of nowhere, saddled to a woman and her four kids, raising beef to eat. He could do it. He had the knowledge, the contacts, the drive, and the determination. He'd have the money it would take to transform this place from a ramshackle spread to a profitable one with a solid reputation.

Regardless if this wasn't his first choice in life, he was gonna give a commitment, and he was gonna stick to that commitment.

He gave the old head one more solid pat then moved on. The other two horses didn't show the quality of breed the old guy had, but they probably worked for the kids. He doubted Elaine used them on the ranch. There were more stalls, but most were filled with junk—old parts and pieces, a couple tires, a tractor hood, something that looked a lot like an old CAT motor, boards, rusty nails, and old fencing. Nothing worth keeping to him, but he'd guess it's where Elaine went when she needed to fix something.

The snow had covered the yard and ground around the barn, but he wondered if there might be junk lying around out there, too. Come spring, he'd find out.

While he was down in the barn, he mucked out the horses' stalls and gave them fresh water and hay.

"Hey! There he is!" a childish voice yelled as he threw the last of the hay into the last stall.

"Don't scare the horses, son." Elaine's smooth voice came from the shadows.

Then she said, "There are lights here." A scraping sound then a pounding. The lights flicked on. "It's not a switch, though. You have to shove the breaker in."

Somehow that didn't surprise him. He looked over his shoulder at where she stood under a box. An old piece of baler twine looped down. He jerked his head. "I'll keep it in mind."

"It's dark for a long time in the winter. You'll need the lights." She walked away, her steps somehow graceful despite the drooping of her shoulders.

His heart twitched. He could admire a woman who worked hard. Who wouldn't quit. Surely she'd been tempted to sell this place, take her kids, and walk away.

"I'm Gabe. I'm eight." A little boy with a big beanie hat and a thick jacket stood in front of him with his hand out.

Rem bit back a smile at the serious look on the little face and took his hand, pumping it up and down. "I'm Rem. I'm thirty."

Out of the corner of his eye, he saw Elaine's head jerk, like she hadn't known how old he was. Or maybe she was worried he was going to eat her son after they shook hands.

"Mom said you might marry her and stay here."

"If that's what she decides she wants."

"Well, Dad left. Mom says she doesn't know why." Gabe opened his mouth to say more, but he didn't get a chance.

"Gabriel. Find out if Mr. Martinez gave the horses grain. You can talk later, after the work's done." She rustled around over in the corner of the barn. Rem wasn't sure what she was doing, but she had the little boy that had gone in to go to the restroom the night they met at the gas station with her.

"I gave them hay and water and cleaned their stalls."

Gabe jerked his head up then started chattering about how much grain they gave and why, where it was, and other details that Rem filed away. He worked the whole time he chattered. Rem had a feeling his mother wouldn't take kindly to him standing around. He liked that. He could handle kids of any caliber, but he appreciated that these had been learning to work and didn't seem to feel entitled.

Gabe chattered most of the next two hours while they fed and watered. Elaine gave occasional instructions, and a few times, she spoke to the child that worked at her side. Rem wasn't sure of his name.

Once they were on the barn floor, he saw two old four-wheelers, although only one looked like it had been used in the last ten years. There was also a snowmobile. He'd never actually seen one of those up close, but he'd seen them on TV and in magazines.

"It doesn't work." Elaine's voice sent a fluid shiver down his spine.

She wasn't short, and with her heavy jacket on, she wasn't as thin-looking as she seemed inside. Her cheeks were red from the cold, and her blue eyes sparkled. Her hair was mostly hidden by her hat. She had her hands in her pockets and stood casually, neither showing disinterest or a desire to be too close.

After being chased for so many years by the young women who followed the rodeos, it felt almost odd to just stand casually and chat about a broken snowmobile.

"I've never actually been around one before, but I can sometimes fix things." He'd actually been pretty good at piecing things together. Growing up, his dad had big dreams and in the early years, not enough money to make it all work.

"That'd be nice." She didn't move to go, studying him like she might find answers to her questions in his stance.

"There's a shed over there." He nodded his head in the direction he'd seen a building sitting off by itself. Not big enough to be an equipment shed, it was too large and not the right shape for a chicken coop.

"There's a big lake on our property." She pointed north. "My grandparents and great-grandparents used to do a lot of ice fishing. They used that shed to keep their equipment but mostly to clean and cure the fish. I think part of it was a smokehouse." She paused. "It's been a while since I was over that way, but there were a couple small cabins. Nothing fancy, but I guess they were built for friends who came and fished. I haven't thought of the lake in a while. Too busy with other things."

Rem nodded, interested that she'd had the ground in her family for so long. No wonder she didn't want to lose it.

"There's only fifty-two head of cattle, and they're all here. I always count them, just to make sure." She turned her head as the boys yelled, jumping from hay bale to hay bale in the loft.

"Yeah. I'll be sure to do that." Rem turned to face her more fully. "I don't want to impose on your supper, so I'm going to head out."

"You're not imposing," she said quickly. Her tongue came out, and she touched her lip.

Rem's eye caught on it, and he watched, fascinated, for a couple of seconds before he realized what he was doing and tore his eyes away.

"I read over the report after you walked out. I don't need any more time to make a decision." Her chin tilted up. "I'm ready if you are."

The inside of his chest felt like a bucking bull that had lost its rhythm. His hands started to sweat, and his vision tunneled, the way it did just before he nodded his head to open the gate.

He flexed his fingers inside his gloves. There was always that little temptation there, the idea that he could quit. Get off. Up until he nodded his head, there was always an out. Not that he'd take it, but it was there.

Same for this.

He'd never chickened out. Not on a bull's back. He wasn't starting here.

"I'll tell Ford. He'll bring the preacher out tomorrow morning. What time will we be done feeding?"

"I start at five, and I'm done by seven."

"I'll tell him to be here at eight. That'll give us time to eat breakfast."

Chapter 5

Elaine stood at the stove, stirring the gravy. Behind her, Heaven helped Carson set the table. A plate clanked. Then the lighter click of silverware. A glass.

The comforting smell of roast beef colored the air, with the softer tones of butter and mashed potatoes filling in the edges.

The heat from the stove felt good after being out in the cold.

Gabriel and Elijah were fighting over who had to clean up the basket of clothes that had just gotten knocked over. And Banjo, their dog, never one to waste an opportunity to put his mark on something that was clean, had burrowed into the clothes, prompting a hide-and-seek game.

It was a typical evening in her home.

Except there was a dark-haired, black-eyed Texan sitting at her table. If the ache between her shoulder blades was any indication, he was staring at her.

Normally, she might have music playing, or she'd be laughing with Heaven over something the baby did, or she might try to put Banjo in the mudroom until the ice had melted off his fur and he was dry.

But not tonight.

Tonight, she felt like she had a ball of barbed wire in her stomach, and despite the warmth of the steaming gravy, her fingertips were cold.

She wanted to pat her hair. Maybe put on something a little nicer than the t-shirt that she'd had since before the kids were born and the old jeans that had blown out both knees, plus the spot that had caught on an old rusty nail halfway up her thigh.

Or put on shoes, rather than standing in front of the stove in her old gray socks that used to be white, with one big toe sticking out of the hole at the end. Wouldn't be too bad, except the last time she'd painted them had been about three months ago, so half the nail had chipped green paint on it. The other half…didn't. All her toes were covered in the other sock, but her heel stuck out.

The cowboy behind her had new jeans on. His socks were white. His flannel shirt was neatly tucked into his jeans, and it fit his broad shoulders perfectly. There were no holes in any of his clothes.

Maybe he wouldn't want her touching his laundry.

Was she going to do his laundry?

Actually, the bigger question in her head was, where was he going to sleep?

Two bedrooms and a bath upstairs. The three boys were in one, Heaven in the other.

Downstairs there was a living room and a small bedroom in addition to the kitchen along with a nice sized bathroom with a tub and toilet, but it also held the washer and dryer.

She spun around. "I can move upstairs into Heaven's room."

He'd been looking at her, but he didn't flinch or look away. "No."

She gathered all the spit in her mouth and tried to swallow, turning back around to the gravy that had started to boil two minutes ago.

Supper was ready. Unfortunately, she was not.

It was tempting to list all the stupid decisions that had led to this point in her life. The biggest being her marriage to James when she was twenty. People had said she was too young. She didn't agree with that, because she'd still be married to him if he hadn't left.

When Remington Martinez was twenty, he'd spent a month in jail for disorderly conduct, public drunkenness, and resisting arrest.

When she was twenty-two, Gabriel had been born.

When Rem was twenty-two, he'd spent six months in jail. Driving while under the influence and totaling a 2010 Mustang.

At that point, the report said that he gave up drinking completely, based on interviews with friends and acquaintances. No one else had been involved in his accident, but he could have killed someone that night.

"Okay, kids. Wash your hands and sit down."

The kids ran to the sink. They always listened better when she called them for supper than when she told them it was time for bed. After James left, something that she had needed to learn was to discipline them and train them to obey. There was no way she could raise four kids on her own if they didn't listen.

Despite their high energy—they were kids after all, not robots—and the chaos in her home, her kids usually listened the first time.

At the time she'd been figuring out how to train them, it had kept her mind occupied. Now, having kids that listened kept her sane.

Gabe had grabbed Carson and put him in the high chair. Elaine turned the gravy off and grabbed the pot handle. She knew before she turned that Rem was behind her.

"You just put everything on the table in the pans?"

"Yes." She'd long ago stopped using serving bowls except for Christmas. Why dirty two dishes?

He grabbed the potatoes and the roast. She'd been betting that he was a meat and potatoes guy, but now she wondered if his tastes might run more toward spicy food. Tacos, chilis, and whatever else they ate in Texas. BBQ. Her children and she weren't used to stuff like that, but she could learn to cook it.

Her spices included salt, pepper, and ketchup. That was the total lineup.

Something told her Rem might want her to expand her spice rack.

She set the creamed peas on and noticed that Gabe was pulling the end chair back. When James left, Gabe, all of six years old, had taken his place at the end of the table. She'd moved to the other end with the baby beside her on her left. Heaven and Elijah sat on the right side.

With a look at the table, Elaine grabbed the high chair and slid it down, moving the empty chair beside it to the spot beside the end she usually sat at, giving the head of the table to Rem. She wasn't a feminist. Never had been, but the last two years had taught her clear as day that she didn't want to have all the responsibility. Didn't want to make all the decisions. Didn't want to be solely responsible for the pile of bills, for calling the doctor in the middle of the night, for deciding when an animal was too sick to get better and needed to be put down.

She'd been there. And it sucked.

Rem could have the head of the table. She'd share the responsibility, or she'd give it to him. But she was worn out from shouldering it all herself. Being in charge wasn't the most important thing. Not to her.

His sharp eyes missed nothing as she pulled her own chair out and sat.

She looked up at him, ready to see an arrogant smirk or even a smart comment. But she encountered neither.

Instead he seemed to be trying to figure her out. Or maybe, as he looked at the head of the table and all the eyes that stared back at him, he possibly had a little respect in his eyes for the chair and the work and responsibility it represented.

Regardless, his hesitation only lasted a fraction of a second; she'd have missed it if she weren't watching for his reaction. He pulled the chair out and sat down, looking at all the blond-haired, blue-eyed people staring back at him.

Finally his gaze rested on Elaine. "Do I say the blessing?"

Normally she made the children take turns for breakfast and dinner and she said it at the supper table. But hope had stirred in her breast at his question. Not only because that question, combined with his getting married in front of the preacher comment, gave her hope that he respected, if not loved, her God, but also because coming on the heels of him realizing what she was giving him by seating him at the head of the table, he hadn't needed to ask her.

But he had deferred to her, anyway.

It was possible that she wasn't marrying a tyrant.

"Yes," she said, more because she wanted to hear him pray than because she thought he ought to do it.

He didn't flinch. "Let's pray." His low drawl warmed her heart as the proud, dark head bowed, bending to the idea that there was Someone greater than he in the universe, willingly giving the respect and honor due such a Being.

"Lord God, I thank you for this table, this food, and this family. Bless the hands that raised it and prepared it. Give us nourishment and rest, and may any glory be yours in the name of Jesus. Amen."

He lifted his head, his eyes searching for hers immediately as though wanting her reaction.

Elaine realized with a start that she'd spent the whole prayer staring at Rem and had neither bowed her head nor closed her eyes. Her cheeks heated.

On a normal day, her children would have called her out for not giving God the respect he deserved by a head bowed in homage. But they seemed cowed by the dark cowboy and were unusually quiet.

Elaine picked up the roast and handed it first to Rem.

He took it, picking up the serving fork and looking at Elijah on his right. "How much do you usually get?"

Elijah's blue eyes widened, but his mouth stayed closed.

"Just a small bit," Elaine said. "He can get more if he finishes that." She was sure she had enough meat cooked, despite the large serving Rem put on his plate before passing the roast to Heaven.

Ford had kept her supplied with meat when she didn't have a steer of her own to eat. She always had the butcher cut the roasts in big pieces when she had a beef done. Not only were the butchering fees cheaper, but she'd use leftovers for roast beef sandwiches tomorrow or stew.

She eyed the amount of meat Rem put on his plate. There might not be leftovers today. She scooped out enough potatoes for herself and Carson then passed them on, trying not to stare at Rem's big, dark hands. How could she not stare? Those were the hands of a man who could turn this ranch into a profitable operation. Strong hands.

She passed him the peas. He gave them a dismissive look and started to pass them on, then he stopped. Glanced around at all the faces staring back at him. His lips twitched, and he pulled the pan back, grabbing a scoop.

"You want peas, bud?"

Elijah looked at Elaine.

She raised a brow at him. "You can tell him the truth, but you're still eating a helping."

"No, sir. I don't," Elijah said.

Rem snorted and shot a sideways glance at Elaine. They shared a smile. Her heart trembled.

His brows lifted before he turned back to Elijah and, without a word, dumped a small scoop of peas on his plate. He handed the pan off to Heaven, who actually liked peas and took two helpings.

Rem dug in without saying much. Elaine didn't expect him to. In her experience, men didn't mess around with their food. Her children were quiet, too. Much quieter than usual. That was a relief, except if Rem were going to lose his temper with them or if childish noise was going to be something that annoyed him and caused him to leave, she'd rather know it now.

Even though her rational mind knew pretty much anyone could fake it for one evening.

It didn't take long to eat.

"Gabe, you take Elijah and finish folding those clothes." Elaine pushed back from the table. "It's your turn to help clear the table and do the dishes, Heaven."

Rem stood as well. "That was the best meal I've had in a long time. What can I do?"

"You don't need to help," Elaine said as she wrung out a cloth to wipe Carson's face. "We've got it."

Rem didn't say anything. Heaven stacked the plates. He carried the pots to the counter then started water running in the sink.

Elaine had her back to him as she wiped the mashed potatoes off Carson's face.

"So, am I washing?" he asked.

She turned sharply, but he was looking down at Heaven who gazed up at him with almost hero worship, nodding.

Fear rolled over in Elaine's stomach. Would her children be able to handle falling in love with another man then having that man leave like their father did? She didn't want to put them through that, wanted to protect them.

Of course she knew that she couldn't protect them from everything and that they needed to experience bumps and bruises in life in order to learn and grow and become stronger people, but parents were supposed to be the constant through a child's life while those bumps and bruises were happening. Not the ones causing them.

Behind her, Rem carried on a low conversation with Heaven, who answered in monosyllables while she carried dirty dishes to the small counter. He didn't talk to her like a kid, which Elaine thought was good, but she suspected that he hadn't been around kids much.

Finished wiping Carson, she set him down. He toddled over to Banjo who had made short work of any crumbs that fell from the table. She smiled as Carson grabbed the dog in a big hug, chattering away as toddlers did. It was times like this, seeing how happy her son was and how good Banjo was with him, that made all the messes she cleaned up because of the dog worthwhile.

She made short work of wiping his high chair and putting it away. Hesitating because she was still not used to the sight of a man standing at her sink, she moved over.

"I'll finish here, Heaven. You go put your clothes away."

Heaven set the last glass on the counter and hurried into the room with her brothers.

Taking a deep breath, Elaine stepped to the counter and glanced over the leftovers.

"It's been a while since I washed dishes. People mostly have dishwashers nowadays," Rem said. His shirt sleeves were rolled up to his elbows. His forearms were brown as they disappeared into the water. The twisting muscles fascinated her.

His head turned, maybe to see why her hands had stilled. Her eyes snapped to his, and her neck heated. She hadn't meant to stare at his arms.

She begged her brain to grind into gear. What had he said?

"A dishwasher is on my wish list, but I'm not holding my breath to get one anytime soon." There were a hundred other things that would actually be considered necessities. Like fencing to keep her cattle in. Groceries.

"I don't mind washing dishes," she said. If he didn't want to, she could finish. "It gives me a little time to think. Usually the kids are scarce when I'm doing it."

"They're probably afraid you'll rope 'em into finishing up if they show their faces." He put another plate in the drainboard and didn't show any signs of stopping.

"That's exactly right," she agreed, surprised that her uneasiness had ~~eased~~ faded somewhat. She was marrying this man in the morning. She didn't expect to be relaxed tonight.

But as she moved around, gathering the things she needed to turn the leftovers into shepherd's pie, she found the splash of the dishwater and his casual movements relaxing indeed. Especially combined with the chatter of her children in the other room.

"I'd better remind them they're supposed to be folding those clothes and putting them away."

"Yeah, kind of sounds like they might be burying the dog."

Almost to the living room doorway, she stopped. "I'll make sure that doesn't happen to your clothes."

He rinsed off a plate, his hands shiny wet and brown. No less tough-looking as they handled the cheap glass. "I'm not worried about it. If this is the way winter is up here, I doubt I'll see anyone 'til spring anyway."

"We see folks at church on Sundays if we get the feeding done in time."

"I'll see that it gets done." Their eyes met.

Something seemed to pass in the air between them. Something hot, and Elaine felt something a little dangerous, too. But it made the tension drain out of her shoulders. Maybe some that he was planning on going to church, would make sure they went. But more that the burden no longer rested squarely on her.

Her lips turned up, and she nodded once before going into the room.

Chapter 6

Rem watched Ford's SUV pull into Elaine's driveway. It wasn't as chilly this morning as it felt last night, but maybe that was because the wind wasn't as strong.

Elaine had been there to greet him when he arrived at five this morning. They'd fed, then she'd cooked breakfast while he showered. He supposed it should have been the other way around, but she was getting ready now.

The brewing tornado in his stomach had been unexpected, so he'd walked out onto the old, ramshackle porch to watch the sunrise over the snowy flatland.

This was supposed to be a business proposition. He'd intended to keep his marriage vows, of course. He didn't give his word lightly. But he'd thought he'd just stay detached from Elaine and her children.

When Ford had mentioned this idea, it was the ranch and the money that interested him. He hadn't even cared what Elaine had looked like. Hadn't expected to see a slender woman with perfect curves. Hair the color of wheat straw that hadn't been rained on. Eyes that evoked the same emotions he felt when he looked at the sky of his home state.

Emotions. He wasn't supposed to be feeling emotions.

He'd thought they could be friends. He'd seen plenty of marriages with less. Although, in today's world, most people with less divorced to try again with someone else rather than put up with, or fix, what they had.

Everyone was on their best behavior last night, including Elaine. He had to remind himself of that. He hadn't been expecting to like her. Hadn't been expecting this thread of attraction that tugged at his body when she stood near. He snorted. She didn't even have to be standing near. His eyes sought her out wherever she was, ran down her back and over the curve of her hip.

But it was her smile, when the tiredness fell from her face and it transformed into something that made his heart hurt to look at, that caused him to wonder if this whole situation might be more dangerous to his sanity than he'd figured.

Olivia's betrayal had hurt his pride. Her actions had hurt his heart. He'd thought she'd been different than the rodeo bunnies that followed the circuit. But she'd gone where the money was, same as every other woman he'd ever known. Even his mom had left his dad when things had gotten tough. She'd come back after his bull riding money had turned the ranch around.

Somehow he'd still held out hope that there'd be a woman who would stand beside him, working alongside him.

After Olivia's betrayal, he'd decided he'd rather have that than whatever fleeting high love brought.

That's what he'd thought he might have with Elaine. No emotions. Just a side-by-side working together. Maybe a comradery.

Not love. Not this annoying attraction that he felt when he was in the same room as her.

Ford's SUV pulled to a stop. Morgan sat beside him in the front, and Rem assumed it was the preacher getting out the back. An older gentleman with gray hair, casually dressed in jeans and a Carhart coat. No hat. Man, these northerners were crazy. He'd walked outside with just his flannel shirt on, and he'd have gone back in almost as soon as he came out, except the closer it got to their wedding, the more awkward he'd felt around Elaine. He didn't want to walk in and see her. What would he say? What did one say to a woman on her wedding day when he'd just met her the day before?

Guess he'd better figure it out pretty quick, because Ford, Morgan, and the preacher weren't gonna be here long.

"Hey, Rem. It's a nice warm morning to watch the sun come up." Ford grinned as he followed Morgan and the preacher up the steps.

Rem huffed. His breath immediately froze into a big white cloud that drifted off on the chill air. No Texan in his right mind would consider this warm. This was what hell looked like when it froze over.

Rem nodded at Morgan when she greeted him. Then his eyes went to the gray-haired man behind her.

"I'm Pastor Houpe." The preacher held out his hand. "This isn't something I normally would agree to." His lips turned down, and he slanted a glance at the closed door. "But Ford assures me you intend to keep your vows and that woman needs more than I can do for her."

"Yes, sir. I don't give my word lightly, and especially on a vow made before God."

The old man studied Rem with one eye narrowed a bit more than the other. Finally he nodded. "You can't judge a man by what you see. Only God sees the heart. But I trust Ford. I also have a peace about this marriage that truly surprises me." He pressed his lips together. "I think you're going to be good for Elaine and her children. But—" Here, he paused and seemed to peer deep inside, seeing things, maybe, that Rem would prefer to stay hidden. "I also think that maybe Elaine will be good for you. I think you might need her."

That rubbed him the wrong way. "Don't want to be disrespectful, pastor, and don't want you to think I don't respect women. I do. And from what I've seen, I like Elaine. She does real good for herself. But I'm never gonna need a woman."

"Never is an awful long time." The pastor clasped his hands over the book in front of him and rocked back on his heels.

Rem was saved from answering by the opening of the door. Elijah and Gabe spilled out onto the porch, Banjo shaking it as he came behind them. The smell of cinnamon and yeasty bread flowed out like water in a trough.

"Mr. Ford! Miss Morgan!" they hollered as they threw themselves into Ford's and Morgan's arms.

Rem knew his friend had lost a leg in the accident that also marred his face and hand, but he kept his balance easily and swung Elijah up in his arms.

A bit of jealousy pinched Rem's skin as he watched how the boy smiled and hugged Ford. He pushed it aside quickly. He wanted respect out of the children and their mother. Not love. Nothing mushy-gushy that would hurt if they left him.

They walked into the house. Rem held the door on the pretense of being polite, but honestly, he was just putting off seeing Elaine.

They'd worked pretty much in silence this morning, other than her instructions when he needed to be told what to do. They'd eaten breakfast the same way.

And he wasn't sure what to say to her now. So he took the easy way out and avoided her. At least until everyone else had walked in. Then he had no choice. It was like sliding down on the back of the bull. He wasn't completely committed yet, but he was that much closer to the head nod that would open the gate.

He walked in the door.

Elaine stood at the head of the table, facing them, her hand on the back of the chair that he'd sat in last night at supper and again this morning at breakfast.

Her slender neck worked as she swallowed, but her small chin was up and her face composed.

Her porcelain white shoulders were exposed in a dress that was more like summer than Christmas. White with big yellow flowers on it. There was no cleavage, but it cinched her waist then flared out around her hips and fell in flirty waves of material that swirled around her legs as the baby at her feet shuffled around her with his arms raised.

Her hair flowed around her shoulders in loose waves, longer than he'd thought but every bit the white blond that was as opposite to his as it could be.

Morgan moved behind him, and he barely noticed her until she pulled the door out of his slack hand and shut it.

His face heated, and he was grateful for his sun-darkened skin that hid his flush. What was he thinking, standing in the doorway staring at her like he'd never seen a woman in a dress with her hair down before?

He'd seen plenty. Plenty of women. Plenty of dresses. Plenty of hair.

So why did this woman, in this dress, with this hair stop him faster than a solid metal gate?

He shook his head. "I guess we can get this over with. I've got some work I'd like to get done before dinner."

The soft look in her eyes disappeared as he said it, and he regretted his words immediately. But the pastor had just talked about him needing Elaine, and for a few seconds there, some emptiness in his soul that he hadn't even realized he had begged for the woman on the other side of the table. It felt an awful lot like a need. And there was no way Rem was ever going to need anyone again. Especially a woman.

"That's probably a good idea. I have some hospital visits to make once we're done here." The pastor shuffled forward, his book in hand. "Do you have any place in particular you want to do this? Maybe beside the Christmas tree?"

"No. Right here's fine," Rem said.

Morgan's brows lowered, and her fingers tightened on Ford's arm. Rem ignored her. He wasn't here to please Ford's wife. He hadn't even thought about pleasing the woman who was soon to be his own wife. His collar suddenly felt stifling, and he couldn't wait to get this over with so he could unbutton the top button. He hadn't noticed he'd gotten the wrong size when he took the tag off this morning.

"I don't have a tree." Elaine's voice flowed smooth as honey. "But the kids and I decorated a spot in the living room."

Her face ticked up a notch, and he realized she was challenging him. They stared at each other across the table.

So, their first fight would be in front of the preacher and their neighbors. If that's the way she wanted to play it.

Some part of him said since he didn't care where they got married, and she did, he should give in.

But he did care. He didn't want to make more out of it than what it was. When she started getting dressed up in fancy dresses that fluttered around her legs like silk on a prayer, and when she let her hair down so that it flowed over her shoulders more beautiful than any horse's mane, and when all that made his fingers itch to touch her to see if she was as soft as she looked… Yeah. He cared.

She broke eye contact first, turning to the stove and grabbing a hot pad before pulling warm cinnamon rolls out of the oven along with something that looked and smelled like apple crisp. He might have been able to hold up, but after closing the oven door, she opened the freezer and set a container of vanilla ice cream on the counter to thaw.

He'd marry her in a suit and tie in New York City with ten thousand people looking on if that's what he had to look forward to eating after he said "I do."

"If she made a spot in the living room, let's use it." He waited ~~e hooked his hat on the peg~~ beside the door while everyone else filed out of the kitchen.

He waited for Elaine to go past him.

"Thank you," she said.

The look of triumph he expected to see in her eyes wasn't there. He was familiar with that look from Olivia. Any time she got her way, she notched a win. And she kept score.

But Elaine gave him a soft smile as she passed. If her lips trembled a little, if her hands were clenched in front of her, if her eyes were slightly pinched, he didn't really notice.

He did, however, notice that she was in her bare feet.

He swallowed at the sight of the pink toes, feeling like he'd just tightened his bull rope and rubbed it good to get the rosin hot and sticky, seconds away from it being too late to turn back.

Still, once he'd gone that far, he'd not gotten off until the bull had thrown him. Unless he made a full ride. It had been called the longest eight seconds in sports, but somehow he doubted it compared to the lifetime he was about to pledge.

Chapter 7

Elaine's hands shook as she picked up the bouquet of poinsettias Heaven and she had put together this morning. They were fake. As was the greenery that she'd wrapped around the window, threading it with white lights and red berries.

A Christmas tree had been more than she could handle with all four kids and all the outside work. If they'd had a fake one, she would have put it up, but she couldn't afford to buy one. Not this year.

Still, the living room looked festive. And clean. It wouldn't stay that way for long, but all the toys were put away, and there weren't any clothes or dog bones, and the mud had been scrubbed off the old hardwood floor.

She had the small coffee table with their lone manger scene in front of the window that she'd decorated. Maybe they wouldn't be standing in front of the altar, but they could exchange their vows in front of the manger. The altar and church setting hadn't helped James remember that he was supposed to keep the vows he'd made, anyway.

"Is this the right spot?" Pastor Houpe asked, stopping in front of the coffee table.

"Yes." Her voice came out lower and more husky than usual. It didn't tremble. She was grateful for that.

Her boys wrestled a little, but they stood where she'd instructed last night when she'd gone over what was going to happen with her kids. Heaven stood on her side. Carson still wanted her to carry him, but she'd been resisting. Something about being married to one man while holding the child of another just didn't sit right, no matter how much the second marriage might be a business arrangement and not a real love match.

She'd tried the love match. It hadn't worked.

Surely this couldn't be worse?

It could. She was sure of it. There was always "worse." But at least there wouldn't be the money struggles she'd had with James. Maybe that had been part of the problem, although she'd not seen it at first. She hadn't minded staying at the ranch. James, on the other hand, couldn't stand working from sunup to sundown with no break other than church on Sunday.

The problem hadn't been her.

Maybe one day she'd believe that.

Very conscious of the man behind her, she stopped in front of the pastor. Ford and Morgan stood back some, in front of the couch, and Rem strode confidently to his place on the other side of the preacher, facing her.

He was tall and big and even now had the beginnings of a cocky grin lifting a corner of his mouth. Not a grin that said he thought things were funny. But a grin that said he'd take on the world by himself, and he might not make it, but he'd laugh while he was doing it, and he'd die trying. It was a look that impressed her. Made her feel like maybe she was making the right choice.

If he were bothered or the slightest bit nervous, she couldn't tell.

"Clasp right hands, please." Pastor Houpe's scratchy voice startled her. For once, her kids were quiet, but before she could lift her hand, Carson stumbled into her leg with both hands up.

"Up, up," he said, his hands thumping against her dress. The swirl of material made her notice her bare feet, which she'd thought were as appropriate as flip-flops. She didn't have any other shoes that would go with this dress. The only winter clothes she had were a black skirt and several different tops that she wore with it.

She hadn't wanted to wear black to her wedding, business arrangement or no.

Morgan stepped forward to take Carson, but Rem swooped him up, sticking him in his left arm before taking Elaine's right hand in his.

Carson still hadn't decided if he liked the dark stranger, but he wasn't shy like Heaven and Elijah. Maybe he liked the view from his new, higher position. Whatever it was, he stuck his thumb in his mouth and stared at Rem, quiet.

"I've got him," Rem said to Morgan.

Morgan's raised brows said a lot, but she smiled, too.

Elaine hadn't moved. The warm hand that held hers was rough and dry. It infused confidence and strength through hers, although there were also shock waves that pinged like she'd hit her funny bone.

Only she hadn't, and her eyes flew to his in time to see an almost imperceptible widening of his eyes, a twitch of his brow, before his face resumed his half-cocky, half-humorously arrogant look, although this time it was laced with steely determination.

"Go ahead," he said to the preacher. His low drawl combined with the touch of his skin made Elaine want to shift her bare feet on the floor.

Pastor Houpe cleared his throat and began. Elaine had trouble concentrating on anything other than the hand holding hers and the rich, deep drawl of the man in front of her as he pledged to stay with her until he died.

She must have said her vows, too. The pastor had been warned, apparently, that they didn't have rings, because he didn't ask for them. He also didn't mention anything about kissing at the end.

"I now present you to Mr. and Mrs. Remington Martinez."

Ford and Morgan clapped, and Elaine's kids joined in.

It took Elaine a bit of time to shake the daze that she was in. "Everyone can come to the kitchen and sit down at the table, there's sweet rolls, apple crisp, and ice cream."

She didn't give her new husband a glance, although she wanted to, but spun, her dress billowing out, and strode out into the kitchen, concentrating on thinking about the plates and glasses and silverware that she'd need and not about what she'd just done. The voices of the adults behind her—Ford's tones then Rem's laughter—followed her out of the room.

Serving the refreshments should give her something to focus on. Except, instead of finding a place at the table with everyone else, Rem's heat hit her bare arms and shoulders, and she turned to see him beside her.

"What can I do?"

"You can sit. I'll serve you." Did she sound breathless?

His voice was low but firm. "You sit. I'll serve. Or we'll do it together. But I'm not sitting while you keep working. You've already done more than I have this morning."

Her lips pressed together, even while his words sent warmth through her. A part of her hoped it wasn't a show. The bigger part knew that whatever nuances Rem might have in his character, fakeness wasn't one of them.

"I need to set this stuff on the table and get the kids settled."

"You work on the kids. I don't want to see you get anything on your pretty dress."

That same warmth spread and blossomed. How long had it been since anyone cared whether she worked all the time or got her dress dirty? The wedding had done nothing but give her pain in her stomach, but his words gave her a euphoric glow as she settled the kids and chatted with the adults.

The preacher and the Hansons didn't stay long.

Morgan walked out with Pastor Houpe. Ford hung back and waited until they'd stepped off the porch before he glanced at Elaine then Rem, including them both before he spoke. "I think you can get the money moved to your account right away. They'll want you to drive to Fargo and show them your marriage certificate within a certain time."

"You have the number?" Rem's dark eyes were all seriousness when he looked at her.

"It's on the letter." For a while, she'd been able to forget that he only wanted the money and the ranch. This brought it back and spoiled all the good feelings that had been chirping in her chest.

"The money was transferred the day I called." Ford gave them both another long look. "Let me know if you need anything."

"You've already done so much. I truly appreciate it." Elaine wished there was a way she could pay back everything they'd done for her.

Rem shifted. She didn't look directly at him, but she got the impression he was annoyed. Maybe he was impatient to get the money. But it felt more like he didn't want her attention on Ford, which was weird.

"Please tell Morgan I said thanks for everything. And if there's ever anything I can do…"

Ford grinned. "We'll get you to babysit."

Elaine's eyes widened. "You're expecting?"

Ford's smile seemed to burst from his face. "Yeah. We just found out."

"Congratulations! That's great!" Of all the regrets she had, and there were a lot, she didn't regret her children. They were the biggest blessing in her life.

Rem slapped him on the back. "Keep working on it, man. It's gonna take a while for you to catch up to me."

Ford snorted. "Think I'd like to do it one at a time."

"No challenge in that."

Ford laughed. They closed the door behind him.

Maybe it wasn't just the money and ranch. He'd admitted he wanted the challenge too. Somehow that didn't make her feel better.

The kids had been cleaned up and were running around the house.

"You want to get that letter? We'll call before we clean up the food."

"Of course. I'll just be a minute." She spun and hurried into her small bedroom, closing the door behind her. Their guests had been there less than an hour. It was probably dumb of her to even get dressed up. But she had wanted to feel pretty for just a little bit. Maybe she wanted Rem to notice her. He didn't seem to put any effort into looking breathtakingly handsome. While she felt drab and exhausted all the time.

But it hadn't worked. He hadn't sent her any lingering gazes or told her she was beautiful, although he did call her dress pretty.

It was a good thing he liked it because it was her only summer dress and he'd be seeing it every Sunday come summer.

She changed quickly, not allowing herself to wonder where he was going to sleep tonight. James's dresser was still there and empty. There wasn't anything to arrange, just Rem's clothes to move in.

He'd said no when she asked if she should move into Heaven's room.

Pushing those thoughts aside—all they'd do was make her anxious—she grabbed the letter before hurrying back out.

He had the table cleared, and he was wiping it, Carson on his shoulders, when she walked in.

Carson laughed, his chubby hands gripping tight to Rem's cheeks. It had to hurt, but Rem had one hand on the rag and one hand on a plump foot, his fingers tickling the stubby toes.

"Thanks for holding him during the ceremony," she said.

"What's the ex's visitation schedule?" he asked, not acknowledging her appreciation.

She straightened her shoulders, preparing for his reaction. People had told her she was stupid, and maybe she was. "He signed away his rights. I don't get any child support or alimony, but he doesn't have any right to my children."

Rem's hand stilled on the table. He straightened slowly. "He's not giving you any money?"

"No."

"Was your lawyer stoned when he made that deal?"

"It wasn't the lawyer. It was me. That's what I wanted."

"You wanted to let him off the hook for his responsibility?"

"No." She looked around to see if any of the older children were listening. She had sworn they would never hear her bad-mouth James. "He left me. Us. All of us. I didn't want to give him any rights to tell me what to do with my children or to do anything with them at all when he couldn't be bothered to even be here." She closed her eyes and sucked a breath in. "I was pregnant with Carson when he left. He didn't come to the hospital. Not for the birth. Not after. He's never even held Carson. He didn't watch the other kids and he didn't take care of the ranch while I was gone. I can't co-parent with someone like that."

Rem stared at her. Whether he thought she was stupid, like everyone else did, or whether he didn't believe her, she couldn't say. There were two sides to every story. Probably James had an excuse that sounded reasonable. And probably her reaction to ask for him to sign away his rights in return for not having to pay her anything was extreme.

Maybe her children deserved their father and she should have fought to force him to be one. She could be wrong—she'd been wrong about so much in her life—but fatherhood just didn't seem like a job that could be forced. Either he wanted to, or he didn't. Since he didn't, she felt she was better off on her own.

Rem finally turned, shaking the rag out in the sink and rinsing it off with one hand. He lay it on the counter and turned.

With Carson still on his shoulders, he asked, "You want to call or you want me to?"

"I'd better do it. The letter is addressed to me." She went to the shelf where she kept her purse and pulled her phone out. "Do you want to see it first?" She held the letter out.

He took it silently. It didn't take him long to read it. There wasn't much there. Basically, she had six months from the date of the letter to get married. If she did, she would inherit a billion dollars. It was hard to comprehend that much money, but the letter was clear.

They had to stay and settle in North Dakota. They had to show their original marriage certificate to the lawyer in Fargo. And they had to stay married. If they broke the conditions, they were required to pay the money back.

He handed it back to her. "It looks like a scam, but Ford said it was legit."

She nodded then punched the number into her phone. It wasn't every day that she called a lawyer, but she wasn't nervous. However, when no one answered, but the phone continued to ring, unease tightened like a lasso around her chest.

She let it ring until an automated voice told her to hang up or try her call again.

Her eyes slid to Rem's. She pushed her lips up but was pretty sure he wasn't fooled into thinking she was smiling while she punched the number in a second time.

Same result.

Pushing the red button, she let her hand drop to her side and faced the man across the table.

"Maybe they're off for Christmas." She wanted to phrase it like a suggestion, but her voice sounded weedy.

Rem glanced at his own phone. "It's a little early for lunch, but that's a possibility, too."

"I guess I'll just keep trying." Careful to keep her exterior calm and unruffled, Elaine squirmed like a bucket of worms on the inside. If the number was legitimate, there should be a way to leave a message, an answering service, something that said she'd called a lawyer's office.

The small number of times she'd dealt with the lawyer during her divorce, she'd never called and not gotten *something*.

She walked over and turned the faucet on, getting water to wash the dishes.

"I'm sorry I didn't have a ring." Rem's voice penetrated the haze and fear that had taken hold of her. If the letter turned out to be a scam, would he leave right away? Would she be dealing with another divorce? Maybe he'd wait until spring to go.

"It doesn't matter. A ring didn't make any difference before." She caught the bitterness in her tone and hated it.

Carson squealed as Rem lifted him over his head and set him down. Elaine figured he'd want right back up, but he ran on his stubby legs into the living room.

Rem touched her arm. "I'm not him."

"I'm sorry. I guess it's been kind of a stressful day." And it wasn't even dinnertime yet.

"I've got some work to do in the barn. I want to fix the snowmobile. Then I'd like to check out the property if you have time to show me. Not today." He moved away from the sink and started putting his boots on.

"I'll have dinner ready at one rather than twelve, since we just ate."

"That's fine."

"Can I go too?" Gabe came out of the living room and stood, a little hesitantly, in the doorway.

"You come out with me, I'm putting you to work."

"Yeah!" He jumped, punching the air, then ran for his winter clothes.

Elaine almost rolled her eyes, even as her heart pinched. He was so desperate for a man's attention even work sounded good. Although he was still at that age when most work was still fun because it was new and better than school or doing dishes or folding clothes.

"You don't have to take him if you don't want."

Rem paused in lacing up his left boot. "They're not going to learn how to work like a man if I'm too busy to be bothered with them."

How could he make her whole chest feel hot and tight and good with just one sentence?

She swallowed around the lump in her throat. "Thanks."

Chapter 8

The weather was bad on Sunday, so they didn't make it to church. The church Elaine usually went to wasn't Pastor Houpe's church but was due south from her ranch.

By Monday, the snow had stopped, and Rem had told Elaine he'd do the afternoon chores so she could take the kids to the special New Year's Eve celebration in town where, apparently, they were having an old-fashioned supper auction.

He'd seen Elaine work unselfishly, and he wanted her to have some time to mingle and work with the other ladies in town. Something she would never have been able to do before he came.

Gabe had assured him that last year when they'd done this, most of the dinners had gone for less than five bucks. So, while Elaine was bathing the baby, Rem had handed him a ten and told him to make sure that he bought his mother's meal, just in case Rem didn't make it there in time.

He glanced at the clock on the pickup console. It would be started, but he imagined that Elaine probably would set her package of food back when she saw that he wasn't there.

He thought.

He'd been doing a lot of thinking lately. Especially since Elaine hadn't gotten an answer any time she'd called the lawyer.

He supposed that would be God's idea of a joke if there wasn't any money after all. First, he sank all the money he'd earned riding bulls into his father's ranch with the understanding that it would be his someday. But his brother got it. Or would get it, since his dad had cut Rem out of the will.

Then he married for money, which he knew he shouldn't have done, and there wasn't actually any money. Just a ranch that needed funds desperately.

He snorted. Irony was always best when it was in someone else's life.

He had some savings. Working on the fishing boat had paid well, and he'd saved it all. But it wasn't enough to do everything that needed to be done on Elaine's spread.

He stretched his neck to the left then the right. Normally it was stiff, but sleeping on the couch made it even more so. He'd thought adding on or building a new house with a separate bedroom for himself would be one of his first projects. If the money didn't come through, that wasn't going to happen.

He started through Blandburg, a quaint town with snow piled up on both sides of the street. One main street with shops, some occupied, some obviously not, and a few houses lining either side. The white church was at the end, and he pulled into the full parking lot. Elaine had mentioned it was a popular fundraiser for the whole town. It was held at the church, but it was a community affair.

Even though he'd told Elaine that he'd get up and do the work in the morning, she'd still gotten up and come out. They'd worked side by side, and he had to admit he enjoyed it. She wasn't talkative, but somehow she complemented him in a way he wasn't expecting.

His stomach rumbled. The woman could cook, too.

His feelings of family and home, warmth and companionship were unexpected. But he'd finally decided that it was okay for him to like her. They could be friends. It wasn't a major catastrophe if they got along well. He just wasn't going to depend on her. Wasn't going to get any strong feelings involved.

He sniffed the cold air as the wind blew past. Yeah, he thought he could smell the fudge brownie cheesecake that she'd baked that morning. Man, it had smelled good. He put his hand on the doorknob and pulled.

~~~

Elaine stood beside Nell Eastler at the front of the crowd. Normally Nell didn't make it to most community activities, either, since she had been responsible for taking care of her sick mother. But her mother had passed away this past fall.

Currently Karen King's box was being auctioned. Nell's was next.

Then Elaine's.

Elaine tried to glance around inconspicuously, but Rem had not showed up yet. She figured he'd text if he wasn't going to make it, but they hadn't agreed on that, and she didn't know him well enough to say for sure.

She really wanted him to be here. She wasn't going to question why.

Around her, the crowd cheered as Karen's box set a new high for the day. Fifteen dollars. Of course, Karen was a young, unmarried woman, one of the few in her twenties, so there were several men bidding against her brothers.

The men laughed good-naturedly as one of the brothers pulled a twenty out and waved it around. "I could get better food down at the feed mill, but I can't let Austin Westly sit with my sister." He waved the twenty at the auctioneer. "I'm bidding it all."

The crowd laughed. Karen, standing by the auctioneer's side, said, "I'll remember that tomorrow when you come in for dinner. I'll just send you straight down to the feed mill."

"It's closed on New Year's," her brother said with a wink.

"Exactly," Karen said, to the laughter of the folks standing around. "That'll teach you to say the feed mill is better."

Everyone knew Karen was an excellent cook and took the good-natured bantering between the siblings in the lighthearted way it was meant.

Eventually her basket sold for forty-five dollars, and she stuck her tongue out at her brother before taking Austin's arm and skipping off with him.

Nell was next. Nell wasn't a flashing beauty, but she was happy and fun, always with a smile. Several of the boys in the Sunday school class that she used to teach started bidding on her right away.

Elaine was laughing at some of their antics when Gabe pulled at her hand.

"Mom?" he whispered.

She leaned down, grateful that several older ladies had taken the younger children to the activity room to keep them entertained during the auction.

"What, honey?"

"Rem gave me ten dollars to bid on your box for him if he didn't make it, but I left it at home." He bit his lip, and his fingers twisted together.

Her heart sank. She couldn't replace his money. She had five dollars in her purse, but it needed to go into her gas tank to get them home. "It's okay." She glanced beyond the auctioneer at the door. "I'm sure he'll be here soon, anyway."

"But your box is next. And I don't know if he had more money."

That was a conversation she needed to have with him. Her bank account was nearly empty, and the lawyer's office hadn't answered the phone any time she'd called. She'd known this when she married him, that her time was almost up with her money almost gone. She needed to sell a cow, which is what she'd been doing to make ends meet. Unless he had a better idea. Either way, it was something they needed to talk about. But conversations about money were never easy, and she'd been putting this one off. She wasn't even sure he was going to stay if the money from the inheritance didn't come through.

"If you don't have it, you don't have it. I suppose this will help you be more responsible for the next time, but for now, there's nothing we can do." She gave him a soft smile to ease the sting her words might have caused.

His sweet hazel eyes held hope. "Do you have money?"

She bit the inside of her cheek, forcing her lips to turn up, not wanting him to see how much her answer distressed her. She shook her head. "Only five dollars, and I need it for gas."

His lips twisted and straightened, and he turned his head away.

She hated disappointing her kids. It might be good for them to learn about being frugal, and even better for them to not get everything they wanted, but it seemed like those were two lessons she taught her children multiple times every single day.

The crowd cheered, and the preteen boy with the winning bid walked smiling up to the auctioneer, handing out his ten-dollar bill.

The boxes were going for more than they'd gone for last year, too. Not for the first time, she wondered if Rem even had any money. Maybe that ten dollars was the last ten bucks he had.

The auctioneer slid her box to the front, and she walked forward, giving Nell a smile as she did.

A murmuring went through the crowd, because she was even there, when she usually wasn't, or maybe because they were wondering who would even bid on her—a woman with four small children. A man would have to be crazy to want to be stuck with her.

Or well-paid.

Rem was supposed to be well-paid.

Up until this point, she'd wanted the billion dollars for herself and her kids and to save the ranch she loved, figuring there would be plenty to share and not minding doing it. This was the first time that she said a prayer that the money would be there for Rem. He deserved it for taking a risk that no one else would take.

"Who will give me a dollar?" the auctioneer asked.

The silence screamed louder than the North Dakota wind in a thunderstorm.

Elaine tried to find something to look at, something to keep her from making eye contact with any pitying looks in the crowd. Someone would probably take mercy on her and bid. But they knew they'd be eating with a divorcee and all four of her kids. She didn't think it was arrogant of her to think that she was well-liked in the community. But there was always this undertone of suspicion. After all, James was a nice guy. What had Elaine done to him to make him leave? And with her own sister, of all people.

It was probably only seconds that she stood there in the silence, waiting for one of the hardworking people in the congregation to shell out a dollar for her food. At least they knew the food would be good.

But no one spoke, and the seconds ticked on.

"Fifty cents. Who will give me fifty cents?" the auctioneer asked.

Elaine's face heated as the crowd shuffled. No one spoke.

She hadn't told anyone that she'd gotten married. She wasn't wearing a ring. But normally she didn't have to tell people what was going on in her life. Her kids did it for her. Could that be it? Now, not only was she divorced from a really nice guy, and not only did she have four very energetic children, and not only was she poor as dirt and completely worn out, but now she had a husband who didn't even bother to show up to community functions with her.

Her imagination was running away with her. Of course it was. Whose wouldn't when they were standing in front of a crowd and no one would even give fifty cents for a meal that they'd have to share with her and her kids.

Her hands started to sweat, and it took a deliberate act of self-control to not wring them in front of her.

Pretty soon, the auctioneer would start offering to pay people to take her food.

A gust of wind swept through the church, and she shivered. Or maybe she just shivered because it was so hard to keep standing when she wanted to run.

Against her will, her eyes sought out Gabe. Tears pricked at the back of her throat when she saw his clenched fists and helpless expression. He'd bid for her if he could.

With almost no effort, she pushed the tears away. She'd become very good at pretending she didn't feel like crying. Who would have guessed such a talent would come in handy?

Maybe she should have worn something other than the jeans and flannel shirt she had on along with her winter boots. But if she had to shovel her car out of the snow, since it had just snowed yesterday and was blowing badly, she hadn't wanted to do it in dress clothes.

She'd showered but hadn't had time to fix her hair, which was thrown in a ponytail, and she was sure whatever makeup she owned, if she could even find it, was dried out. All she had were three bottles of nail polish. She bought herself one nice bottle of polish each year on her birthday each of the first three years she'd been married. After that, they hadn't had the money for gifts. James wasn't much for giving presents.

"Twenty-five. Who will give twenty-five cents?" The auctioneer sounded as desperate as she felt. But she kept her head up and her shoulders back. Her entire being hurt with the pain of not being wanted. She couldn't control that. But she could control how much of that pain she allowed to show.

None.

Heavy footsteps clicked behind her.

"Fifty bucks."

"Sold!" The auctioneer hit the gavel on the table so hard the handle broke. "Oh. Wait. Elaine, do you know this man?"

Elaine turned to look at Rem as he finished striding toward the auctioneer. He wore his cowboy hat. His dark hair curled out along the sides. Work boots. Jeans. A flannel shirt that was tucked in.

"It's my husband," Elaine said through lips that felt numb.

Rem stopped beside the auctioneer with his hand out. "Rem Martinez. I got to smell all that stuff cooking this morning, and I can't wait to eat it." They shook hands.

The auctioneer, William Bruckner, picked up the box. "Boy, it does smell good."

"I'm so hungry my stomach's gnawed a hole in my backbone. That meatloaf and scalloped potatoes is gonna go down fast."

William sniffed again. "I smell chocolate."

"Fudge brownie cheesecake," Rem said with a look of anticipation, like he'd eaten it a million times before and loved it.

He'd told her just this morning he'd never had it.

Rem shifted the box into one hand, gave William a fifty-dollar bill, and grabbed Elaine's hand. "We gonna round up the kiddos and go eat?"

It was funny how much time she'd spent holding back tears of sadness, loneliness, pain, and despair. She'd gotten so good it hardly took a thought. But this new feeling—what even was it? She didn't know, but it overwhelmed her, hitting her with the force of an out-of-control tractor, and she couldn't stop the pooling in her eyes or the tightening of her chest.

She put her head down and walked swiftly out of the room, toward the hall where the activity room was. She hadn't even thought about Gabe until she heard his light footsteps behind them and his voice calling, "Mom, wait."

The restrooms were just ahead. She swerved to hit the ladies' room, trying to tug her hand from Rem's grip.

He didn't let go.

Her tears spilled over.

"Here, Gabe. Take this." Rustling was loud in the hall as he handed the box over.

"What's wrong with Mom?" Gabe asked, his voice heavy with worry.

"I'm gonna find out," Rem said with calm assurance. "You take this and get us seats. You can get your brothers and sister if you're allowed. We'll be out in just a minute."

A sob backed up in her throat, and she shoved her fist over her mouth to keep it from coming out and echoing in the hallway.

Gabe's footsteps faded away.

The ladies' room's door was just in front of her. She tried tugging her hand out of his again, but he didn't let it go.

"If you're going in there, I'm coming in with you." Rem's tone held a warning.

Praying that she could keep her voice level, she said, "I just need a minute."

He pushed open the door to the Sunday school classroom, pulling her in and closing it behind them.

She was able to pull her hand free from his, and she swiped at her face before she wrapped both arms around her stomach.

He shifted behind her, then there was no sound other than the ticking of the old clock on the wall.

She was grateful for the silence and for the time. Even if he pressed, she wasn't sure what she could say was wrong. Was she crying in relief? Was it just the effect of standing in front of a crowd and being faced with the fact that no one wanted her and her children? Not even for a paltry fifty cents?

The people weren't being mean. She knew they weren't. Everyone was just waiting for someone else to step up and do the charitable thing.

She was sick of charity.

Sick of being the one no one wanted.

Sick of being the one that never had enough, couldn't keep her husband, and needed her neighbors to provide Christmas presents for her kids. She snorted. Now, she couldn't even sell the stupid ranch, because Rem had married her to get it.

"Elaine?"

He was probably worried she'd gone crazy on him. Maybe she had.

"I suppose if someone had offered them a billion dollars, they would have taken me." She hated the bitterness that erupted from inside. "I'm sorry. That was my worst side coming out."

"That's okay. We'll starve it into submission." His stomach growled.

She chuckled and brushed the rest of the tears off her cheeks. "I'm sorry."

"You said that once already. I said it was okay. I meant it." Rem's easy drawl flowed across her bruised emotions like a cheek against the downy softness of a newborn baby.

"No. You've done nothing to deserve my anger or my bitterness. I'll try to do better." She turned. "You know, for the first time today, I wanted that billion dollars, not just for us, but for you. Because you took us when no one else wanted us."

His mouth was open, and he stared at her without blinking. Like he didn't know what to make of her. Probably he didn't. They'd not even been married for a week. He was the one who hadn't gotten what he'd wanted, but here she was crying and snapping at him for no reason.

She blew out a breath. "Okay. I'm ready. Sorry for the drama."

She started to walk, but he moved, quicker than she'd thought he could, and took her shoulders.

"I don't know what to say to that, Elaine, because it's true. I married you for the money and the ranch. But I hate that it hurts you."

"It doesn't. I was having a pity party, but now it's over. I don't know why I even said it. I wanted you to marry me, and I knew it was for the money and the ranch." She tilted her head. The light in the room was dim, and she could only see shades of gray, although his eyes were black and shrouded as he stared down at her.

The heat from his large hands made her body burn.

"You only married me so you could save the ranch and get the money."

She bit her lips and nodded. "That's true." Her throat felt tight, and she tried to swallow through it before she spoke. "Thank you for taking a chance on us. I hope you don't regret it."

"I don't have regrets. In order to regret anything, I'd have to stop moving forward and turn around and look. Not doing it. I like the challenge, and I'm pretty excited about meeting it. I'm happy." His hands loosened on her arms, and it was almost like they rubbed up and down a fraction. "I can't change the truth, though."

She had herself back under control. Whatever that sweeping of emotion was had disappeared, and she was back to being able to face reality without the irritation of her emotions getting in the way. "You don't need to. It is what it is. I do, however," she said, surprised that her lips tilted up, "appreciate you paying fifty bucks for me. You walked in at the perfect moment."

He lifted a shoulder and gave a grin, his teeth gleaming white in the dimness. "What can I say? I have good timing." His stomach rumbled again.

"Ready to eat?"

"Let's go, then. I might have married you for your money, but that's only because I hadn't tasted your cooking."

She laughed. She could joke about that. "I thought you'd like the spicy stuff. You know, tacos and chilis and all that."

"I do." He opened the door. "We definitely need to get hot sauce out at the house."

"You might have to order that online. I'm not sure grocery stores in North Dakota stock hot sauce." They did, of course, but she gave him a sassy grin.

"Maybe I'll have to do that. I kinda like it when my food bites back." He closed the door. "But your stuff's good without it." He took her hand. She wasn't sure why he did. They'd just established, again, that their marriage was a business proposition. But he took it, and she didn't pull it away.

"I think you'll eat anything that doesn't eat you first."

"No way. You saw how fast I slapped my fifty bucks down. I wasn't taking a chance on any other lady's cooking."

She snorted. "I don't get the whole hot sauce thing, anyway. It's sadistic. Why would you want to be in pain while you eat?"

"I'm in constant pain. Plus, hot sauce doesn't hurt. It just gives a kick."

She stopped. He stopped beside her, his smile turning to confusion.

"You're in constant pain?"

His face cleared, and he lifted one broad shoulder. "I don't think about it."

"From bull riding."

"Yeah."

"You were good?"

"Yeah."

Normally she did think of him as a little cocky. A little arrogant. But that answer actually sounded humble.

She wanted to ask, to find out more about him, but they needed to get in to her children. So, instead, she said, "I'd like to hear about it sometime."

They walked into the fellowship hall. Elaine felt like the conversation died down when she walked in holding Rem's hand. Whether it was because everyone was so surprised that someone would have the guts to marry her, or whether it was because Rem was such a commanding figure, she wasn't sure.

Tall and handsome, his confidence practically oozed off him. They were probably a striking couple, too. With his dark handsomeness next to her light blond hair. Although he was good-looking in an almost sinfully rich way, and she was…plain.

"Hey, Mom! I saved you guys a seat." Gabe waved them over from the other side of the room.

With a complete lack of self-consciousness, Rem strode between the tables.

"Hey." George Wittacker, a middle-aged store owner, stopped them. "You Remington Martinez, the championship bull rider?"

"Yeah." Rem jerked his head up.

"Thought so. I seen you on TV. Ain't no one can ride like you." He stood and held his hand out. "Honored to meet you."

Rem shook his hand, keeping Elaine's hand in his left.

Jen, his wife, shook her head. "We were watching when that bull, Endurance, pitched you against the gate and cracked the back of your skull open."

Elaine felt her mouth drop as her eyes went to Rem's head. He always took his hat off when he came in the house, and she'd noticed his straight black hair more than once. Noted that it was a little longer than she'd prefer. But looking at it now, she realized she'd never noticed the way his hair didn't quite lay flat along the back of his head. That must be where the scar line was.

"We thought you was a goner." George looked at Jen for confirmation. They nodded together. Several other people at the table concurred.

"We saw the replay a couple of nights later. I can't believe you didn't die." Hannah, sitting across the table from George and Jen, took a sip of her water bottle.

Rem started to move off.

"You two really get married?" George asked.

"Yep. Last week," Rem said.

"I didn't even know you two was seeing each other." Hannah narrowed her eyes like Elaine had kept it hidden on purpose.

"Well, it happened kind of fast…" Elaine started.

"She's a woman worth settling down for." Rem gave one of his cocky grins and tugged at Elaine's hand. "I've never met a woman that can cook like her. Never knew how nice it would be to walk in from the barn in the morning to the smell of fresh baked cinnamon rolls and frying bacon."

Now she knew he was laying it on thick. She'd never once stayed in the house and cooked while he fed by himself in the morning.

"She is a good cook," George said, giving Jen a sideways glance, like he wasn't sure if he would offend her by admitting that.

"She works hard, and she's easy on the eyes. I'm a lucky man."

Rem moved away. Elaine followed without comment. Until they were out of earshot.

"I've never baked or cooked while you were out doing the work in the morning."

"Didn't say you did."

"You said you never knew how nice it would be to walk in from the barn…" Elaine's voice trailed off. He *hadn't* said she did. "I think that's kind of like lying."

They had almost reached the table where her kids where. Rem stopped and leaned his head down to her ear. "No. It's not even close. But this town has no idea what you're worth."

"I was supposed to be worth a billion dollars," she muttered.

"I'm not talking about money. I'm talking about your work ethic. Your cooking and baking abilities. Your determination and perseverance. They look at you and see a woman whose husband left her with four kids, and they think there's something wrong with you, when they're the ones that were misled."

She glowed under his praise, even if it was kind of backhanded.

Maybe this business proposition was exactly what she needed.

Chapter 9

The Saturday after New Year's, Rem lingered at the dinner table. Normally, he'd been spending most of his time outside from before breakfast until after supper.

"I'd like to talk to you for a minute after you put the kids down for a nap." He rose as she wiped Carson's face off. "I'll do the dishes."

Her face registered surprise, but she nodded. "Heaven and Gabe, you make sure you have all your schoolbooks gathered up. You go back on Monday. Then you two can play quietly in the living room until Rem is ready to go back outside."

She hadn't blinked an eye about the kids going outside with him. In fact, she seemed pleased that he would take the time to talk to them and teach them. It still felt kind of odd, because he'd never really given kids much thought before he'd married Elaine. Sometimes they made his work harder, but most of the time, it was fun to have someone to talk to, and for some reason, they both seemed to worship him.

He was washing the last dish when Elaine came back down the stairs after putting Carson and Elijah down for their naps. She came over to the counter and started putting the food away.

He rinsed the dish off and let the water out, drying his hands.

Ever since he'd seen her cry at the auction, he'd been thinking differently about Elaine. She was tough, no doubt. Having four children and surviving alone here on the ranch. He couldn't imagine doing it all himself.

But under that tough layer, that ability to survive and thrive in harsh conditions, there was a vulnerability there, a softness that matched her delicate looks. It attracted him. Made him feel like he was needed—she needed him. His protection, his help, his support…he wasn't sure what, exactly, but whatever it was, he wanted to give it to her.

She could need him. That was okay. As long as he didn't start to depend on her.

He took a hold of her wrist, slender in his hand, and he had to force himself to just hold it, because his fingers wanted to slide up her soft skin.

She glanced up, her blue eyes wide.

"You heard the kids talking about it at dinner; I got the snowmobile running today."

Her eyes sparkled. "They were so excited. It was nice of you to take them for a ride." She lifted a shoulder. "I know you did it more for you to ride out and check the cattle than for us to have a good time on."

"It was my pleasure. I'd never ridden one before. It's a lot of fun."

Her smile widened. "It's even better at night with a full moon on the snow."

He watched her face beam, her eyes shine from the simple joy of remembering riding over the snow. His heart thumped in his chest, and suddenly his hand was doing what he'd not wanted it to do, sliding up her arm, feeling its warmth and softness.

Her eyes darkened, just enough to make his breath hitch and something quiver in the air around them as his finger reached her elbow and he allowed it to continue up, skimming over the soft material of her t-shirt and on to the warm softness of her neck. Her skin was delicate, and the contrast with his rough finger fascinated him. He watched as it traced over the scattered pulse in her neck before his hand spread and he cupped her cheek. Her head tilted and pressed into his palm. His other hand itched to touch too, but he swallowed, torn. This wasn't the type of relationship he wanted with her. They were friends. Business partners.

But he was touching her like a lover. And she was letting him. Enjoying it, if her half-closed eyes and racing heart rate were any indication.

His body wanted to press forward, but his brain told him he was being stupid.

"Mom?"

Elaine's eyes popped open, and her head straightened. Rem dropped his hand as she turned toward her son.

"Yes?" she asked, her voice even more husky than usual. It curled around his heart. He wanted it soft and low next to his ear while her fingers skimmed over his back...

"Can Heaven and I get the Legos out if we promise to clean them up when we're done?"

Rem stepped in. "Yes. You can. I'm going to take your mother for a snowmobile ride. She'll give you her phone, and I'll have mine. We won't be far away, and you call us if the kids upstairs wake up or if anyone comes."

He'd been going to ask her if she wanted to go for a ride with him, but after whatever moment they'd just had, he hadn't wanted to risk her saying no. He told himself it was because he wanted to see the ranch boundaries, but he knew that was a lie. He wanted her to be with him.

Elaine got her phone and gave it to Gabe, giving him the same instructions he had probably heard a thousand times as she went out to the barn to feed and take care of the stock.

The color in her cheeks was high as she ducked her head and went to the door to get her winter things on.

Rem wanted to grin at her sudden shyness, except he felt the same way. What had they been doing?

He didn't need to ask. He'd been seconds away from kissing her. Still wanted to, actually, as his eyes followed the lines of her body, graceful slender curves, delicate features, soft, fragrant skin. Brown sugar and vanilla. He could smell it still.

Suddenly he realized she was ready to go out, and he'd been standing in the middle of the kitchen staring at her.

He strode over to the door, annoyed with himself. The stupidest thing he could do right now was fall in love with his wife. He'd been stabbed in the back too many times by people he loved and trusted. The only way to protect himself was to keep an objective distance between them.

After what her ex-husband had done, Elaine knew it too. He was confident she felt the same. They would both be working to hold themselves back.

~~~

Elaine followed Rem to the snowmobile that was parked in front of the barn. She'd grabbed her sunglasses from her car, and Rem had on a pair of mirror shades that made him look like a movie star on TV. Not the look she needed to see right now after she'd almost begged him to kiss her in her kitchen just a few minutes ago.

Bad move on her part. Not only was she living up to the love-starved divorcee cliché, but she didn't want to ruin the business arrangement they had going. Most of all, she didn't want to fall for a guy that was going to leave, and so far, they'd not gotten a hold of the lawyer, and they had no idea if they were even going to get the money she was supposed to have inherited. Without that, his leaving was a certainty.

And why would she want to kiss a man who wasn't even here for her but for the money and the ranch?

Man, she was dumb sometimes.

She stood back while he yanked on the pull rope and started the machine.

He got on first, and she climbed on behind him. There was no way to not be close. Her front pressed into his back, and the only way for her to hold on was to grab him around the waist. Through the thick layers of their coats and insulated pants, it should have been impossible to feel heat or hardness. But she felt both.

"I know we can't see all the ranch boundaries, but I was hoping to get a little feel for it," he said over his shoulder in a voice loud enough she could hear it over the rumbling of the machine.

"How about we go see the lake?" It was pretty with some trees and a few little one-room cabins. They were probably pretty rundown now. She hadn't been out in several years.

He nodded, and she pointed in the right direction.

It was a short ride, less than ten minutes, and the lake appeared, flat white and stretching off into the distance. The cabins sat along the lower shore, and Rem took the snowmobile down the snow-covered trail, motoring to the first one then stopping and cutting the motor.

They stared in silence at the expanse of frozen water. The cloudless blue sky above and the brown of the cabins the only color other than a few evergreen trees, their branches laden with snow. A few animal tracks, deer, rabbits, and a few cayotes, marred the glistening perfection of the snow. It was quiet and still. Peaceful.

"I know about a hundred guys who would love to spend a week at a place like this," Rem said softly.

"There's no way to cook in the cabins." Elaine's voice imitated his pitch, like if they spoke loudly, they'd break the spell of the beauty that shimmered around them.

"Bathrooms?"

"No running water. I think about twenty years ago, my grandfather put holding tanks in for the toilets."

"Yeah, make that two hundred. This place is perfect for guys that want to step out of the craziness of civilization."

"You can invite anyone you want to stay, of course." It was as much his as it was hers. "I can cook for them."

"You already do enough." He said it with finality, as though there was no discussion. They hadn't known each other that long, but she'd already figured out that when he felt something was in her best interest, he used commands rather than requests.

"It wouldn't be that hard to throw an extra pan of sweet rolls in the oven and put a couple of sandwiches together along with a jar of soup."

He turned and looked at her over his shoulder. "I'm not inviting anyone here that's going to make more work for you. You have enough."

She pressed her lips together, unwilling to get into an argument and spoil their ride. Not to mention he was right. She'd been exhausted since before she could even remember. If she slept for a solid ten years, she doubted she'd be caught up.

"Mind if I take a few minutes to look inside?"

"Not at all. I'll come, too."

The cabins were just like she remembered. A bed and a table. A small room in the back with a toilet seat over a holding tank. Nothing fancy.

"There's no heat," Rem said.

"I think they used kerosene heaters if they needed them. Some guys didn't use anything, if I remember correctly."

"Talk about rugged." Rem snorted. "There's something appealing about it."

It was the challenge that appealed to Rem. Elaine could have told him that. That's part of the reason that she wasn't even sure he'd stay even if they did get the money. Conquer one thing, move on to something else.

They didn't stay much longer, and didn't go on to see more of the ranch, but drove straight back to the house, each quiet and alone with their own thoughts.

Chapter 10

Monday, Gabe and Heaven went back to school, the cows got out, and the water froze. It was almost five before Elaine remembered about calling the lawyer while she was cooking supper. The two older kids were out with Rem while he did the evening feeding.

A woman picked up on the second ring. "Peregrine Law Offices and Petting Zoo."

"May I speak to Mr. Peregrine, please?" Relief that it was an actual number and an actual lawyer's office overshadowed any concern that the place was also, apparently, a petting zoo.

"He is out with an unexpected medical condition," the secretary said, not unkindly. "And won't be back in for several weeks."

"I have a letter stating I have inherited money from Sweet Water Ranch owner, Mr. Edwards. Is there anyone else I can talk to?"

"I'm sorry. Mr. Peregrine is the only lawyer in the firm. I can put your name on the list and have him call you when he returns to the office."

Was there anything else she could do? She couldn't think of another question she could ask that might get her the money faster, so she agreed to receive a phone call and hung up.

What was Rem going to say about that? A couple of weeks to wait for their money. The lady hadn't said they weren't getting it. Maybe Elaine had been raised not to count her chickens before they hatched, because until that money was in her account, she was going to have trouble believing that it was coming.

She was trying something a little new, a little spicier, for supper. She'd never really eaten or made Mexican food before, and Rem hadn't complained about anything she'd made. On the contrary, he seemed to like it all and didn't hesitate to say so. But she couldn't shake the idea that, coming from west Texas, he was used to something a little different than her normal meals. Not to mention he'd said he liked his food to kick back when he ate it.

A little before six, Rem, Gabe, and Heaven burst through the door, laughing and shaking snow off their clothes. Elaine stood against the counter and smiled with them as they laughed about the expression on one old cow's face as she looked at the patch job they'd done on the fence.

Rem seemed so relaxed and at ease, like feeding cattle in below zero weather with two small children and coming into a shack of a house afterward was something he'd done all his life. Maybe he was just the kind of man who was comfortable wherever he went.

"Mom, Mom! Rem said he'd do game night with us!" Gabe almost jumped up and down in his excitement.

"It's Monday. That's our game night," Heaven reminded her. Like Elaine wasn't the one who had instigated game night to begin with.

"He's welcome to join us." Elaine's eyes met Rem's over the children's heads.

"I smell peppers and onions and chilis and spices that are making my taste buds dance." The grin hadn't faded from his face, but a look of anticipation had entered his eyes.

"I'm giving it a shot, but it might not be any good."

"It could taste half as good as it smells, and it will be awesome."

It turned out to not be too bad. Rem seemed to like it. Her kids weren't overly fond of the new heat in their food. She'd anticipated that and hadn't put as much spice in as the recipe she'd found online had called for. Plus she'd made sure there was plenty of rice.

Rem's thank you at the end of the meal made the extra effort worthwhile.

The kids loved game night, and they cleaned up the table and kitchen extra quickly. All four of them had gone in to pick up the toys in the living room and spread the Twister sheet out on the floor as Elaine washed the last pot and Rem held a drying towel in his hand.

"You didn't have to make that for me tonight."

"I wish I knew what you liked and how to make it better."

"Elaine, whatever you make is fine. I've loved eating your cooking."

She scrubbed at the crusted-on food. "I know you're used to different food, and it won't hurt us to expand our culinary experiences."

"Well, thanks. I don't expect it, but I appreciate it."

Maybe it was his appreciation. Maybe it was her own satisfaction that she'd done something new and a little hard and been successful at it. Or maybe it was just the cozy atmosphere, the feeling of fun and family, and the easy burn of another day filled with work finished, but Elaine found herself wanting to lean her head on his chest and feel his arms come around her.

She pushed back against the desire, which was almost a longing.

"The lawyer's office answered today."

"Shoot. I totally forgot all about even calling." He snorted, like he couldn't believe he could forget about a billion dollars.

"It's not exactly good news. The lawyer is out for surgery and won't be back in for several weeks. The woman I spoke with couldn't do anything for me except put my name on a list for the lawyer to call when he got back into the office." Her hands continued to scrub, but she took a moment to look at Rem. He wasn't smiling, of course. She couldn't tell what the bunched muscles in his jaw meant.

She hadn't wanted to have the money conversation now, but it seemed like the right time. "I don't expect you to keep us afloat with whatever money you might have. I can call the butcher in Rockerton and—"

"No. It's not going to help anything for you to sell your cows. I have enough in my account to get us through the winter. I probably have enough to do a little more than groceries and regular expenses. I'll get my stuff together, and you get yours, bills, anticipated feed expenses for the rest of the winter, that type of thing, and we'll sit down some evening this week after the kids go to bed and figure it out."

"Okay." Her voice was a little uncertain because she'd expected the conversation to be awkward and uncomfortable—it was money, after all—but Rem seemed to be facing it head-on. Although, he really didn't have to. It wasn't part of their bargain for him to have to support her and her children with his own money.

He put a hand, warm and strong, on her shoulder. "Let's not ruin game night for the kids by worrying about it tonight."

"Are you ready, Mom?" Heaven asked from the doorway.

Elijah ran over and plowed into her, wrapping his arms around her jean-covered legs.

Elaine gave him a one-armed hug before answering Heaven. "Just about. I have this last pan to do. Is the floor cleaned up?"

"Yep."

Five minutes later, Elaine sat in the recliner with Carson on her lap and the spinner in her hand. Elijah and Heaven stood on the mat with one foot on yellow and one foot on blue.

"The winner gets to play Mr. Rem," Heaven said.

"Oh, no," Rem said easily from the doorway where he leaned with one shoulder on the doorframe. "Gabe is next."

"Mr. Rem might not even want to play," Elaine said. Rem hadn't come the whole way into the room, like he was waiting for a chance to duck out. She didn't think he was the kind of guy who wouldn't speak up if he didn't want to do something, but she definitely didn't want him to feel like he had to play.

"Nope. I'll take my turn."

"You can come in and sit down." The couch was where he slept. His blankets and pillow were folded up and set behind it, out of sight. He did that every morning before he left to feed.

"I'm good here. I can see better. I've never played this game, and I need to work out my strategy."

The kids laughed.

Elaine's eyebrows rose. Strategy, for Twister? "Someone doesn't like to lose."

His lips curved up just a little. "That's right."

"Okay, everyone ready?" Elaine spun the dial. The kids always loved Twister, maybe because it was a full body game. There was a lot of laughing and shouting as Elijah and Heaven got into more and more impossible positions.

It was a typical family night for them, except it wasn't. The dark cowboy standing in the doorway changed everything for Elaine. He made the room feel smaller, her skin prickle, and heat come to her face every time their eyes met.

It was different for her children, too. There was a man, not their father, but a man who looked on them with affection, who encouraged them and laughed at their antics. They definitely were showing off some for him.

Heaven easily beat her younger brother, though, and then she faced off with Gabe. Gabe won that round when Heaven put an elbow on the mat trying to stretch across it with one foot on a red spot, one on a green spot, a hand on yellow, and the opposite one on another green.

The game between Rem and Gabe lasted a little longer with Gabe having the obvious advantage of being small and flexible, but Rem had the luck of the spin. Spin being used loosely since it was never really a given what would happen with Carson helping. But everyone knew that's the way it was, since Carson had to be included too, and so no one complained if the spinner went counterclockwise rather than clockwise or if a baby hand stopped it before it stopped itself.

Whatever Elaine called out was the only and final color.

When Gabe fell to the mat, the children yelled and jumped up and down, declaring Rem the winner.

But the dark-eyed cowboy shook his head, his lips pulled partway back in an easy grin. "Nope, I don't think so. Your mother hasn't played yet."

"She never plays. She has to spin," Gabe explained.

"You can hold the baby, and Heaven can spin and call the colors." He shrugged. "I can't be the champion if I haven't beaten everyone."

Elaine's hand had gone to her throat, while her arm tightened on Carson. But her children had gotten into the spirit of the idea, and they bounced around her, begging for her to get up and take on the winner so they could crown a champion for the evening.

This wasn't her game—she was lucky to walk and chew gum at the same time, although it had been so long since she could afford a little luxury like gum the thought was kind of moot.

But the point of family game night was having everyone participate, so she handed a sleepy Carson off to Gabe and gave the spinner to Heaven. Elijah sat on the couch as the only spectator, unless one counted Banjo who lay stretched out on his side beside Elaine's chair.

Already in her stocking feet, Elaine faced Rem across the mat. His mouth tilted in a casual grin, but his stance and the glint in his eye said he was playing to win. Elaine had her share of stubborn determination but not for games where the winner was chosen by luck more than skill. Still, her kids talked in excited voices about who was going to beat whom, and she was going to give it her best shot.

Rem hadn't been a trash-talker all night, but as they bent and put their right hands on green, he leaned a little closer to her and said, "I'll try to make this painless for you."

"I don't think so, cowboy." She reached over and put her left hand on yellow. "I was going to take it easy on you, since it's your first time and all, but forget that."

His eyes flickered, like he'd not been expecting her to sass him. His hand hit the yellow spot beside hers.

"You don't need to go easy on me. I don't want a pity win."

"Oh, this chick is showing no pity." She slapped her hand down on red and smirked at him. His face was close, and his nearness made her heart race. He smelled like strength and the outside, fresh hay and the musky tones of cattle.

Heaven called out green, and she adjusted her foot. Her heart jumped into her throat as his foot crossed hers and claimed the green spot next to her.

He smirked, and his eyes glinted.

She tried not to allow her eyes to widen or her mouth to gape. How was she supposed to concentrate on the game when Rem had his leg practically wrapped around hers?

Pressing her lips together, she tilted her head up and gave him a superior look before waiting for him to put his hand on blue then slapping her hand down on the space closer to him, crossing their arms.

Her move had the unintended consequence of moving their bodies closer together. When, oh when, would she learn to think before she ran into stupid?

But she'd rattled him because he wobbled back on his heels, his arrogant look slipping a bit.

Until the next move when he slid his foot between her legs to claim the yellow spot directly behind her butt.

So she took the yellow spot under his.

Maybe if she hadn't looked at him in order to share a laugh, everything would have gone okay. Whether it was the tilting of her head, or maybe it was him being off-balance, she wasn't sure.

Whatever it was, one of them swayed, and as mixed up as they were, they both went down together, her shoulder under his chest and their legs tangled up like string on a licorice stick.

Her children screamed and laughed at the grown-ups on the floor, but all Elaine could focus on was the hard arms on either side of her and the hot breath on her face. The glinting black eyes had darkened from teasing to something that looked a lot like desire.

Her heart pounded in her throat, and her lips were dry.

She used her tongue to moisten them, and his eyes tracked the movement, heat flaring in them.

His head lowered, and her hand found his shoulder, running lightly over the smooth muscles bunched there.

Her face lifted—if he was going to kiss her, she was going to meet him halfway—then a thump went through both of their bodies, followed quickly by three more. Her children couldn't stand the adults being on the floor by themselves and had hopped on, making a pile of bodies on the Twister mat.

Somehow they all managed to climb on Rem who had adjusted his position so his body covered hers, taking his weight on his elbows and knees, protecting her from flailing hands and feet as the kids wrestled over and around them. Even Heaven was in the fray. Elaine saw her long, blond braid flying.

"Hey, Rem's a bucking bronc!" Gabe called as he swung a leg over and bounced on Rem's back.

Rem rolled, grabbing Gabe and Elijah both and wrestling with them, while Elaine twisted Carson and tried to keep Heaven and him from getting hurt while still letting them feel like they were a part of the action.

There might have been some tickling going on, too. Everyone was laughing and yelling, and there was general pandemonium as Banjo got up and involved, not wanting to be left out.

By the time everyone settled down, Rem was on his side with Elaine leaning against his stomach, Carson on her lap, and the other kids breathing hard and lying either on top of her or Rem. They all took the time to catch their breath while Banjo encircled them, tail wagging, occasionally sniffing them to make sure this was really his family. Family night did not usually degenerate into a free-for-all.

Maybe that was the difference a man made.

Slowly the children's laughter died down. Elaine was acutely conscious of Rem's hard stomach behind her. She wasn't even sure how she ended up that way. It was just a little awkward, even with Elijah's body between them so she couldn't see Rem's head.

Rem hadn't moved since they'd all stopped. In fact, he seemed tense behind her, like maybe he was in pain. Were the kids too hard on him?

She started to move away. That's when she realized that the heat that had been pushing up her chest into her throat was coming from his arm around her waist.

How had that happened?

Her face flushed. He was a handsome man and, with his high profile as a bull rider, was probably used to women throwing themselves at him. She wasn't normally that kind of woman.

She shoved away. "Okay, children. Bedtime."

"Thanks for playing with us, Mr. Rem." Heaven's cheeks were bright red. Elaine couldn't remember the last time her little girl had such a big smile on her face. Her throat tightened.

Now that she was no longer squished against him, Rem was able to get up. The rest of her kids thanked him as they slowly walked out.

Elaine picked up Carson, took at breath, and spoke to Rem's shoulder. "It was awfully nice of you to spend the evening with us."

He didn't say anything. Carson squirmed in her arms. Her eyes slid up until they finally met his.

The cocky grin that usually tilted his lips up was nowhere to be found. His gaze was serious and almost a little humble.

"Thank you for including me in your family night."

Her eyes widened. It was on the tip of her tongue to tell him that he was a part of their family now and of course she would include him, except…he really wasn't.

Once more, the thought slipped through her mind: if the money wasn't there, he probably would leave. Maybe including him had been a bad idea. It could end up hurting her children.

"I have a feeling," she said, "that it will never be fun again without you."

Chapter 11

While Elaine put the kids to bed, Rem shoved his coat on and went outside. He'd never been up the stairs in the house, and although tonight seemed like a good time to start helping with the bedtime routine, he didn't volunteer, and she didn't ask him to, of course.

The big, round thermometer on the porch declared that it was well below zero, and the snow squeaked under his boots as he walked toward the barn.

He must be getting used to the cold, since he felt fine with nothing but his coat on. Funny, because the cold was the thing that bothered him the most when he came.

He didn't really have a destination in mind, just needed to get out for a few minutes, and ended up in the barn by the horses' stalls.

Midnight. That was the name of the old quarter horse in the stall. He snorted, and hay rustled as the big body shifted, coming to the stall's gate and nuzzling Rem's coat.

"Didn't think to bring you anything, old boy," Rem said as he scratched the ears in the dark. He'd spent enough time in the barn that he was comfortable with no lights.

The scent of hay and musky animals, the sounds of big bodies shifting, and even the scratch of mice by the feed bin were comforting and familiar.

Unlike the odd warmth and eddy in his chest that made him feel like he was underwater or too close to the fire. There was no fire and no water, but he couldn't shake the odd feeling.

Partly brought on from playing with the kids, which he'd never done before, the strength of the feeling was caused by more than that.

He hadn't expected to like Elaine.

No. That wasn't quite right. He'd completely expected to like Elaine, at least enough to get along with her. Figured they'd be friends. Figured eventually they'd share a room and a bed, once she'd gotten comfortable with him. That's what married people did, after all.

He hadn't expected to be attracted to her. To feel hot and cold when she was around and have his fingertips tingle with the need to touch her when she was close.

Like she'd been tonight.

How could he not be aware of every move she made? Her smile, the flow of her hair over her shoulder, the arch of her foot.

He'd moved, taking them both down to the Twister mat on purpose because he couldn't stand having her so close and not touching her. Maybe she knew what he'd done. Maybe that was why she had such a hard time looking him in the eye before she'd left the room.

She'd seemed a little shocked, though, at their position when the kids had quit wrestling.

How could he not wrap his arm around her and tuck her into the curve of his body?

He moved his hand down Midnight's furry neck, scratching under the mane.

He wanted to protect her and provide for her, ease her burden and take care of her. He'd wanted that from almost the moment he met her. He understood those feelings and figured that was just the way he was. He'd want that with anyone probably.

But this was more.

It had nothing to do with her struggles and everything to do with how she handled them.

She looked delicate but had that backbone of steel. It wasn't inflexible, though, because she bent gracefully to his will and was somehow able to tell when it was necessary for her to do so and when she could stand up to him.

His phone buzzed, and he welcomed the distraction. He had no idea why he couldn't stop thinking about his wife, but he needed to get her out of his mind. The kind of feelings that were growing inside of him were not appropriate for the kind of marriage they had. They were dangerous, as well, because they would give her the power to hurt him. Like Olivia.

He glanced at his phone before swiping. Ford.

"Hey, man," he said, holding it to his ear while continuing to stroke Midnight.

"Rem, how's married life?"

"Guess I could ask you the same question."

"It's the best thing that's ever happened to me." The slightly amazed note in Ford's voice could leave no doubt as to his sincerity.

"Good to hear. I'm happy for you."

Silence stretched between them. Finally Ford said, "Did you get your money?"

"No. I guess the lawyer had surgery or something."

Ford made a sound of surprise.

Rem told him everything Elaine had said.

"If you need cash to spot you…"

"No." He cut Ford off before he could even go there. If they didn't get the money, it was going to be hard, if not impossible, to keep the ranch. But he wasn't a charity case and would starve to death before he bummed off his friends.

He'd take money if he needed it for Elaine and her kids.

The thought popped into his head, and he knew immediately it was true. He would beg on his knees if Elaine needed something he couldn't provide for her.

He wasn't sure he liked that new discovery about himself. He wasn't even sure it was appropriate, either, considering he hadn't known her that long.

"You seem kind of preoccupied," Ford said. "Where are you?"

"In the barn."

"She's making you sleep in the barn?"

Rem snorted, trying to find the cockiness and self-assurance that seemed to have deserted him this evening.

"No. I came out to check the stock."

"Okay. I'm not going to keep you. I can check into the lawyer and see if he really had surgery, but it doesn't matter how much money I throw around, I'm not going to get anyone to tell me anything about your situation."

"I know. I appreciate knowing I've got you on my side."

"Call if you need anything."

"I will. Appreciate it."

They hung up. It was another hour before Rem made the slow walk back to the house, still not sure what he was going to do. He had this fear in the back of his mind that he was very close to falling in love with his wife.

~~~

Friday night after the supper dishes were cleared, Elaine turned the TV on for her children. There was some kind of rodeo rerun that they found while she was looking for a movie and begged to watch.

It was going to be on for two hours, and it wouldn't contain inappropriate language or sex, so she said okay. Her standards had dropped a good bit. Used to be she tried to make sure their TV time was educational. Now, as long as there were no f-bombs dropping and everyone had their clothes on, she said yes.

When she walked back into the kitchen, Rem already had a stack of papers on the table. "So that's what you do when you need uninterrupted time. You turn the TV on?"

"I'm a horrible mom, aren't I?"

"I think it's kind of smart. If you limit the TV, you can really work it to your advantage."

"You deserve to know what the finances look like, and I don't want the kids to be upset." She pulled her own papers out from where she'd stashed them above the fridge. "Gabe, especially, seems to worry."

"Shows he's not self-centered."

"He's too young to worry."

Rem lifted a shoulder like he didn't agree but wasn't going to argue.

"You think I should dump all this on a young boy?" She almost put her hands on her hips. How could he think Gabe was ready to face this type of pressure?

"Not all of it." Rem seemed to ignore the anger in her voice, since his was just as smooth and easy as it ever was. "He's your kid. Do what you want. I'm just saying a little hardship never hurt anyone, and the boy would benefit from thinking that he was a help around here rather than a baby to be coddled."

"I don't coddle him." Okay, now she was offended. "He and Heaven kept an eye on Carson all the time when I had to go out to feed."

"And it didn't hurt him at all."

"It's too much responsibility for a little boy," she said firmly.

Rem held his hands up. "Your call."

"You disagree."

"I do. The kid's old enough to know that money is tight anyway. You're not hiding that from him. What he doesn't have is any control. He can't help when he doesn't know the problem or solution." He lifted a shoulder. "It's when you don't have control that you feel powerless."

Elaine glared at him from under her lashes, grinding her teeth together. Thinking. His logic made sense, but she just couldn't wrap her head around the idea that Gabe could handle the adult pressures she was facing. She was the parent. She was supposed to protect him.

Rem traced the edge of the papers lying on the table. "You're also keeping him from seeing how you handle this. It's a big problem. Hopefully you're going to stand and fight with courage and integrity. Maybe you'll take some calculated risks. Heck, you already have by marrying me." That cocky grin that made her insides turn to melted butter flashed across his face. "He watches and learns. Or you pull the wool over his eyes and shove him in front of the TV."

"You think Gabe should be out here at the table with us?"

"If he were my kid, I'd want him here. I'd want him to know what was going on, and I'd want him to be part of the solution."

"You'd let your kids know your finances?"

"Maybe not the exact numbers, but yeah. The only time I'd want to hide anything from them would be if I were doing wrong. If I were cheating on their mother, I wouldn't want them to know. If I had a drug problem, I'd hide it." He spread his hands out on the table. "If your life's an open book, it's harder to write the wrong story. The kids'll keep you accountable. It's easier to say no to something that might tempt you because you know they're watching and they'll know."

She thought about Monday night when they'd played Twister. He could have kissed her, and she would have kissed him back in front of the kids.

But that wasn't wrong.

The business arrangement they had for a marriage was more wrong than wanting to kiss her husband on the floor in front of her kids.

She tilted her head. "So, you're not hiding anything?"

His eyes crinkled, and his face seemed to heat under his tan. "I haven't lived the life of a saint. I was in prison, and you know why. Half the bad stuff I've done I was probably too drunk to even remember."

"But you're going to lecture me."

"I wasn't lecturing you." Frustration leaked out of his tone for the first time. "I've watched you. I've heard about you. I've witnessed it myself. Your kids have a great example right here." He tapped the table in front of her. "They could benefit by watching you."

"I'll think about it. But not tonight." She could see his point and even understood. But she wasn't ready to make that change. Wasn't ready to expose her children to the harsh reality that was her life.

He jerked his head up like he understood. "That's fine." He pushed the papers that were in front of him over. "That's a description of the cattle I own in Texas. Eight cows and two bulls. It was a side racket I had in addition to my dad's ranch."

"Side racket?" she asked, glancing over the papers. They didn't make any sense to her.

"An elite bucking bull can go for a pile of money. A big pile. But there's no guarantee a bull'll buck. It can end up being a ton of greenbacks, or it can be a bust." He leaned back in his chair. "It doesn't matter. I'm showing you that because they're part of my assets. I've got a buddy that I'm pretty sure will buy all of them in one shot. He's doing pretty good on the circuit this year, and he's got some money to burn."

"You don't have to sell them. Can't you bring them up here?" There was plenty of grass and no reason why champion bulls couldn't grow in North Dakota.

"I could. Except they're not a sure thing."

"Nothing in agriculture is a sure thing."

"This is worse than the usual. And I can buy fifty head of good beef cattle for what I'll sell these for."

"Oh. I see." She did see. But it almost sounded like he was going to start his own herd on their ranch.

"Yeah." His breath puffed out. "I sank the rest of my bull riding money, everything I got for endorsements, into my dad's ranch. Stupid move on my part since he disowned me."

She couldn't stop her head from yanking up.

He shook his head. "Long story. I was stupid. He was a jerk. That's what it boils down to."

There was pain in his eyes that told there was more to it than that, but she didn't press.

"Just so I'm not stupid again, I want to be clear. I checked the laws in North Dakota. If you divorce me, everything we own is split half and half. I'm not going to lose it all again."

Her eyes narrowed. "I'm not divorcing you."

"I don't think you will."

She noticed that he didn't say he wasn't leaving. It was a question she wanted to ask, especially if they didn't get her inheritance, but she clamped her mouth shut over the words.

He pulled out his phone and did some clicking and typing. He slid it across the table. "Those are my accounts. A business and personal checking and a savings."

She twisted her head to look at the screen.

"Go ahead. Pick it up," he urged. "Look at the accounts. That's everything I'm bringing to the table. We can't make any decisions if you don't know what kind of hand I'm holding."

Gingerly she pulled his phone closer and looked at the screen. It didn't take her long to look through the accounts which contained about thirty thousand dollars total.

He was waiting for her to look up, although he didn't push her to hurry. "I don't have any big bills. Just living expenses, health, and auto insurance. Phone bill. Two grand a month. Most of that's health."

She handed his phone back to him.

He took it from her, their fingers brushing. A casual brush that didn't mean anything. She knew that. But her crazy heart kicked up, and her breath caught at the tingle in her hand.

She filled her lungs and pulled herself together. He'd been very transparent. More than she expected and certainly more than she deserved.

"You've seen the letter." It was on the top of her pile, and she held it up.

He didn't reach for it. "Yeah."

"You know the cattle that I have. Three horses that aren't worth anything. Ten thousand acres with the lake you saw. Maybe a quarter of that on the eastern side is tillable. The rest is pasture and, of course, hay."

She pushed the stack of envelopes in front of her over. Most of it was bills. "I had to take a second mortgage out to pay James off when he divorced me." Because of North Dakota's law where marital property was split fifty-fifty. "The mortgage and second mortgage are the big bills."

She shut her mouth and allowed him to look through everything. He took his time. She wanted to twist in her seat and fiddle with her fingers. She hadn't paid either of last month's mortgages nor January's.

His face probably showed when he realized that, but she didn't watch. Couldn't. She was supposed to have married him then gotten enough money to pay it off. She certainly didn't plan to sit at the table and have to admit that her bills were past due.

But she saved the worst for last.

When he looked up, all traces of humor gone from his eyes, thunderclouds taking its place, she pushed the last two papers over. "Bank statements," she said by way of explanation, although she was sure he didn't need to hear it.

She had three dollars in one account and seventy-two cents in the other.

His body had stilled. She wasn't even sure he was breathing. White-hot anger seemed to roll off him in waves.

Her hands slid under the table and clasped together to keep them from shaking. Rem was finally face-to-face with everything she didn't have, and it was obvious he wasn't happy about it.

James had gotten angry. More than once. But he'd never hit her. She didn't think Rem would, and if he did, if he lifted a finger, she was taking her children and calling the cops. Although he was so big and strong, she supposed she should be more concerned about surviving first.

She was being dramatic, and she knew it. He wasn't going to hit her. Sure as she was sitting here, she knew that.

But his anger, quiet and controlled, billowed thick in the air around them. It seemed to expand and grow, hot and heavy and on the verge of exploding.

He stood so fast his chair flew backward and slammed against the wall with a reverberating crash. He stormed to the door, grabbing his cowboy hat and shoving it down on his head.

"I'm going out," he said, the low tones of his voice completely at odds with the flying chair and his short, angry movements.

He slammed the door on his way out hard enough to knock his coat, which he hadn't taken, and hers to the floor.

Elaine sighed, almost a sob, and put her forehead on her hands.

Three seconds later, the diesel motor in his pickup roared to life. The windows rattled as the engine revved and bellowed, the sound slowly fading away.

He hadn't taken his stuff, not even his coat. He was probably coming back. Although if he were like James, it wouldn't be until morning. She might as well plan on doing the feeding herself when she got up.

"What happened, Mommy?"

She lifted her eyes. All four of her children stood in the kitchen doorway. Eight worried eyes looked first at her, then at the chair that lay on its side against the wall, and finally to the coats that lay in a heap on the floor.

"Did Mr. Rem leave us like Daddy did?" Heaven asked in a soft voice that shook.

Gabe's eyes were just as big and scared as hers, but his chin was up. Elaine thought again of what Rem had said about sharing her problems with the kids. Not so they could handle them for her, but so they could help. And watch how she handled them.

The tears that she'd held back easily when Rem walked out—she wasn't crying over another man, not ever again—pinched in the back of her throat, and her nose tingled.

"No, honey. He just went out for a little bit."

"Daddy always did that too," Gabe said, a hint of bitterness in his little boy tone.

She pushed back away from the table and held her arms open. Carson shoved his siblings aside and came running, his thumb in his mouth and his blanket trailing behind. By the time she had him settled on her lap, her other children had piled on. They all squeezed against her, their little bodies seeking comfort and reassurance by human contact, and again she was hard-pressed to keep her tears in check. But she didn't want her children's memories of her to be constant sobbing every time a man left. She was stronger than that.

She swallowed, the burn in her throat almost more than she could stand.

Maybe she wasn't stronger. She could distract them, though.

"How about I go in and we'll finish watching your rodeo together."

The kids' cries of excitement were a little more subdued than usual, but she knew she'd get them with that, because the only thing better than watching TV was watching TV with Mom.

They settled on the couch, Carson and Elijah on her lap, with Heaven and Gabe snuggled against her sides.

And of course, as life would have it, the next bull rider to come on the screen was a slightly younger version of the man who had just walked out her door.

Chapter 12

Rem gripped the steering wheel tightly, the windows down, letting in the sub-zero North Dakota night. His radio was up as loud as it would go, and his truck hadn't seen double digits on the speedometer since he'd passed the last exit.

That was one nice thing about this frozen hellhole—there was plenty of empty space for a man to work out his anger.

At one twenty, his needle tacked out and his right wheel had a little shimmy. He was angry, not suicidal, so he slowed back down to one ten.

The straight, flat road disappeared past his headlights, the yellow dotted lines blurring together.

He didn't even know where he was going. Nowhere, really. Just needed an outlet for the fury that burned hot and deep inside of him.

He'd never been a brawler, but he'd sure wanted to grab a hold of James.

How could a man treat a woman, his wife, the way that man had treated Elaine?

She'd taken out a second mortgage to give him his half of the ranch. He wasn't paying any support—not for his wife, not for his kids—and Elaine was struggling to even put food on the table.

Rem's hands tightened on the wheel, and his boot had the accelerator floorboarded again. He forced the appendages to relax.

He wasn't going to be able to think about James. Obviously the guy was a jerk who didn't deserve a family like he'd left, but that didn't keep Rem from wanting to punish him for the position in which he'd left his wife and kids.

Elaine was partly to blame. She should have sold the ranch. She could have walked away with a pile of money and no worries.

But Rem could understand the desire to hold on. To have a piece of land one called their own. To work the land one's ancestors worked. Yeah, he got it.

Especially when he figured that Elaine had married James and borne his children under the assumption that they'd work beside each other for the rest of their lives. He was sure she hadn't planned on doing it alone.

He wasn't sure he could see James without feeling the need to rearrange his face, and the hot eruption of anger still bubbled in his chest, but the intensity had lessened. He still wasn't ready to go back, but he needed to.

All those bills and no money. They needed to figure out a plan. Not tonight. It would be too late when he got back. Tomorrow. Soon.

His money was enough to pay most of her bills and keep them through the winter, but they needed some type of income. Something that generated enough to pay the mortgage at least.

Fifty-odd head of cattle with calves by their sides and no feeder steers would keep them for a while, but they were borrowing from their future to sell the cows now.

It was well after one a.m. when Rem pulled his pickup to the barn, hoping that by parking out there it didn't wake any of the kids up.

The light over the stove was on in the kitchen as he sat and took off his boots. Assuming everyone had gone to bed, he went straight to the small bathroom off the kitchen and took a quick shower, throwing his clothes in the hamper and wrapping a towel around his waist before walking into the living room where he kept his clean clothes in his big duffel behind the couch.

Elaine had mentioned that he could use the extra dresser in her room, but he didn't think she was actually ready for that yet.

He was halfway to the couch before his eyes adjusted enough to see that there was a pileup on the couch.

His wife sat in the middle, her children huddled close to her.

Guilt slapped at his heart.

He'd scared them, then he'd left.

He didn't know what James had done, what kind of anger he had shown, but he did know that James had left and never come back.

It hadn't been that long since Rem had arrived in the kids' lives, but he supposed that fear—the fear that someone was leaving, never to return—would live in their hearts for a long time.

He shouldn't have run off, and he'd have to remember that in the future. Although, he doubted he'd ever be quite that angry again. Finding out what a snake Elaine's ex-husband had been had torched his emotions like nothing had for a long time, if ever.

He wouldn't think about why it made him so angry, because then he'd have to admit that he wouldn't be quite as bothered if he didn't care so deeply for Elaine.

Still standing in the middle of the living room, his eyes had adjusted even more while he considered what to do, and he could now see that Elaine's eyes were open and on him.

A sleepy smile hovered on her lips as her eyes ran over his uncovered chest. His heart stumbled at the look on her face.

But then, as though she just woke more fully, her eyes snapped to his, the admiration—if that's what it was—replaced by wariness.

He wanted to go over and bend down in front of her, but he stayed in the middle of the room. "I'm sorry," he whispered. "I shouldn't have left."

"I don't blame you," she said, her voice barely a ribbon of sound. "I don't see how anyone would want to stay and face this."

It took him three seconds to realize that she thought he left because of the lack of money.

He supposed he had, in a way.

Giving in to the desire to touch her, to be closer, he walked over and knelt in front of her, his hand resting lightly on her knee. Because of the rip in her jeans, his fingers touched a little portion of soft, woman skin.

"My anger wasn't about the lack of money or the situation we're in. It was about your ex and the position he left you in."

Her eyes, gray and wide in the dim light, blinked slowly.

"He took half the ranch, Elaine. And he isn't paying a dime. That's not right."

"That's what I wanted."

"Why?" He didn't understand her thinking, not even a little.

"James didn't want us. He didn't want the kids when he left, and he didn't want me, obviously." Her hand slowly ran down Carson's hair, touching it with the love only a mother's hands could show. "I didn't want someone who didn't want us, who could leave us so easily, to have any say in anything I did or didn't do with my kids. But in order for him to give up his rights, I had to sacrifice something. You understand?"

"So you took the second mortgage out and paid your ex for his paternal rights to your kids?"

"Yes. Basically that's what I did. Maybe it was stupid. Maybe I was arrogant to think that my kids didn't need a dad that didn't want them. In fact, I know it was stupid. You know the stupid mistakes you make that seem like the best decision at the time?"

"Yeah." He'd made his share of stupid mistakes.

He stayed where he was for a while, on his knees at her feet, his fingers touching the warm skin of her leg through the rip in her jeans. His fingers itched to move, to slide along the softness, but this probably wasn't the time or place to give in, even a little, to the attraction that tugged at his soul.

A little crazy was in his blood. He couldn't have been a champion bull rider without it. But where people might not understand it, they at least could condone that kind of crazy. The other kind, the kind where he fell in love with this woman and took her kids as his own, no one was going to think he was anything other than full-on, batwing, flipping nuts.

And what woman would want a man that close to insanity?

Chapter 13

The next few weeks slid by. Literally. They had an ice storm that left a glaze on the twenty inches of snow they already had on the ground. Thankfully it wasn't so thick that the cattle, with their split hooves, couldn't break through the crust. However, Rem had never walked on ice before, and he fell a few times before he got the hang of it.

Now he strode in from the barn like an old pro. However, the cold made everything take longer. The water pipe had been frozen this morning, and he'd had to thaw that out before he investigated where the bright red blood on the snow in the barnyard was coming from.

One of the cows had cut her foot on the ice, as far as he could tell. He'd managed to get some disinfectant on it. Elaine's cows weren't wild, but they weren't pets, either.

He shuffled the eight eggs in his hand and opened the door. Ever since he'd said he loved coming into a house that smelled like cinnamon rolls and bacon, Elaine had stayed inside in the morning and had some kind of delicious breakfast ready for him when he walked in. He hadn't known a man could be so blessed.

"Sorry I'm late," he said as he closed the door behind him.

"Not a problem for me, but the kids were sorry they missed you." She was holding Carson on her hip as she cracked an egg with one hand directly into the skillet while Elijah played with a truck on the kitchen floor. Gabe and Heaven would have eaten breakfast before they got on the bus, of course, but Elaine always waited for him before she ate.

"It should be illegal how early those kids get on the bus."

"Before daylight right now," Elaine agreed.

His phone said nine o'clock exactly as he removed it from his pocket and set it on the counter so he could wash his hands.

"Smells good in here." It wasn't just the cinnamon rolls. Elaine had a husky vanilla scent all her own, and he breathed deep as he went behind her to the sink.

"Hopefully it tastes as good as it smells."

He knew it would. He opened his mouth to tell her so, but the ringing of her phone stopped him. He'd only heard it a couple of times before. Each time, it had been her mother reminding her of the birthday party she was planning at their house. Later this week, he thought.

"I'll watch the eggs," he said.

She handed him the spatula while she adjusted Carson on her hip and hurried to her purse to grab her phone.

"I think it's the lawyer," she said before she answered. "Hello?"

His heart thumped in his chest. He was about to become a billionaire. And just in time. He'd spent his own money to buy parts for the tractor and had it torn apart in the barn. He'd seen some good cattle for sale in South Dakota, and if he'd had the money, he'd have added them to their small herd. He was tired of sleeping on the couch, too.

There were a million things he could spend money on, right now. Hopefully they'd move it to their accounts today. Elaine had insisted that they open two accounts. One for him. One for her.

Elaine gave all her information to the lawyer and told him about the letter while Rem flipped the eggs and reached for one of the plates she had sitting on the counter.

"Oh. Are you sure?"

Rem turned at the distress in her voice. She sank into the nearest chair, her mouth hanging open. She let the baby slide to the floor and put her hand on her chest.

Her eyes closed. "Could you look again? Please?" She dropped her forehead into her hand and waited for what seemed like a long time.

Rem's stomach turned over. The hunger pangs that had been squeezing it turned into anxious spasms.

"I see." Elaine took a deep breath, then she seemed to sink farther into her chair. "No. That's fine. Thanks for double-checking."

She hung up. Her shoulders slumped. He thought she might even be crying, but after a few moments, her chest rose and she straightened. Her eyes met his head-on.

"The letter was a mistake. There's no money."

He stared at her. "A mistake?"

"That's what he said. I wasn't supposed to get one. He apologized for his error." She grunted. "I guess everyone makes mistakes." Her head fell back down into her hand.

"That's a pretty big mistake." Rem swore under his breath. A billion-dollar mistake. Which meant that the whole premise that had brought him here was a mistake. A mirage.

His chest squeezed tight, and his neck felt like a lasso had settled around it. No billion dollars. No money at all.

Elaine stood. "Your eggs are burning."

Rem swore again. Louder and more violently this time. He threw the spatula down. It clanked onto the stove. "Guess I'm not hungry anymore." He yanked his coat off the peg and walked out.

~~~

Elaine watched him go, her heart shooting pain around her chest with every hard thump. He'd be leaving now. He'd married her for the ranch, too, but that wasn't any good without the money.

They'd never finished the money conversation from the other night when he'd stormed out. Rem had just given her money without her asking when she said she needed to go grocery shopping. They didn't really need to talk about it, though. They both knew the sorry state of their finances and were depending on that billion-dollar inheritance to save the ranch.

They could last until spring, through summer if he sold his high-dollar rodeo stock, but come fall, they would have no choice but to sell.

She would have no choice.

He had no reason to stay.

She turned the stove off and moved the skillet from the burner. She'd have to clean the burned eggs out of it and start something for dinner. Later.

She put her head on the table, unsure if she were more upset about not actually getting the billion dollars or about the fact that Rem was going to leave.

Having him around had been fun. She'd enjoyed it. But of course, she couldn't deny the attraction that pulled at her every time he was around. He was a handsome, confident man, and a woman would have to be blind to not notice him.

She was sure he liked her too. They were friends. They'd developed an easy comradery. But she wasn't foolish enough to think that he liked her enough to dump all the money he had into a ranch that was going bankrupt anyway and stay with her without the money he'd been promised.

Maybe because she'd lived through James's leaving, brought a newborn home to the ranch with no idea of how she was going to care for him, plus her other children and still pay the bills. Maybe because not having money had become her normal. Or maybe she'd just never really believed that she'd actually be getting a billion dollars. It had seemed too good to be true. Turned out, it was.

Whatever the reason, knowing that she wasn't getting a billion dollars didn't disappoint her like it probably should have.

Glad that her eyes were dry, she stood up from the table, checking her kids before walking to the stove and getting the pan of eggs to clean it.

~~~

Rem stood in the barn, his stomach churning, his mind a jumble, but his heart berating himself for walking out, yet again, on Elaine. It told him he should walk his butt back in that kitchen and face this together, but he'd feel like a big idiot walking out then walking right back in.

He *was* an idiot. Why not feel like one?

He stomped back through the snow, up the porch, and into the house.

If he'd thought about it, he would have expected Elaine to be sitting where she left him, maybe crying or something. But she stood with her back to him, scrubbing the skillet that he'd burned the eggs in.

She looked over her shoulder, her face pinched. "I can get your clothes out of the dryer if you want to leave right away."

He wouldn't have called himself slow, but it did take almost a half-minute until he realized she thought he was back in to collect his stuff and go.

"I don't quit."

She looked down at the floor where her youngest blond-haired boy played with a truck at her feet, before looking back up at him with a raised brow. "I can't quit."

Oh, the words were right there in his mouth to tell her that he couldn't quit on her, either. Not when he wanted to stand beside her for the rest of his life with every fiber of his being.

He shook that thought.

They weren't getting the money. Okay. He wasn't going to sit around and brood about it. He'd told Elaine he didn't look back, and that was the truth. He was ready to forge ahead.

"You have a minute? I have a couple of ideas I want to run by you."

"I'll let this soak," she said, drying her hands off and coming to the table.

He sat at his normal seat at the head of the table. She pulled out her chair to his right. Carson came over with his truck in one hand, his thumb in his mouth, and Rem lifted him up, sitting him on his lap. A few weeks ago that would have felt odd. Now he barely even thought about the fact that the boy wanted to sit in his lap rather than his mother's. The little body on his leg somehow felt right.

He wanted to get the first word in, so he didn't wait for Elaine to settle before he started. "I'm sorry. That was a huge disappointment, but I shouldn't have walked out. That's the second time I've done it to you, and you deserve better. I'll try hard not to let it happen again."

Her head was shaking before he'd finished. "You have every right to be upset. It's the money and the ranch that brought you here. I feel like you've been lied to, and I wish I could change that."

"I'm here. We're married, and I told you I'm not quitting. If you are, you'd better say so."

"I told you I can't." Her eyes slipped to Carson who was running his truck on the table with one hand.

"I get that you're not leaving your kids." He paused, and his voice lowered, losing its hard edge and coming out with a warmth he didn't realize he was capable of. "I'm talking about us. You and me and what we're going to do to keep the ranch and turn it into something profitable. It's going to be work, and it's gonna involve sacrifice, and I want to know if you're in."

She didn't hesitate, and he loved that about her. "I am."

Carson pushed his truck to the edge of the table, where Rem stopped it and pushed it back without thinking about it.

"Do you have any ideas?" He wanted to hear her thoughts before he launched into his own plans.

"I just know I can't keep doing what I've been doing, which is selling a cow every time the checkbook is empty."

"Okay. Here's my idea." He put a hand up. "We don't have to do this. I'm laying it out so we can talk about it."

"I get it."

"I've got a buyer for my cattle in Texas. They're getting some bloodwork done, and if everything comes back clean, that sale should go through by spring. I want to buy as many beef as I can with that money, even if we have to ship them in from back east."

Elaine nodded. That wasn't the radical part of his plan.

"Okay, I know I'm a risk-taker, and this might make you uncomfortable."

Her mouth curved up. "I have to like the part about you that's willing to take a risk."

He returned her grin with a cocky one of his own. Even if they lost the ranch, if he could figure out a way to get Elaine to like him as much as he liked her, he'd consider that risk one of the best he'd ever taken.

"I want to take the money that's in my account, get the bills current, keep back enough to live on for two months, and sink the rest into repairing the cabins."

"The cabins?"

"The ones at the lake."

She looked at him blankly.

"I've got a buddy. He rode bulls for a little bit. I gave him some free lessons and advice, so he kind of owes me. Anyway, he quit a while back, and he and his wife own a vacation booking company. I want to fix the cabins up, get some pics, and see if we can't get some income going from that. Enough to pay the mortgage every month and buy groceries."

Elaine didn't seem excited about the idea, not like he was, but she hadn't said no outright.

"Who would want to come the whole way out here? And there's no place to buy groceries or eat or anything."

"Well, I'm thinking that will be part of the draw. You'll cook for them."

Her mouth formed an "o," and she stared at him.

"Think about it. You don't have to. I know I said I didn't want you to do anything more than what you were already doing. I still don't. But…" He let out a breath. "Come spring, I'm going to have to get a job. Probably in the oil field. They're always begging for guys, so it shouldn't be a problem. Hopefully just for this summer." He hated the thought of leaving Elaine, especially if they were going to have people staying in the cabins.

Elaine bit her lip. Her fingers twisted together. "I won't be able to make enough hay to feed all the stock. It was all I could do to get the little bit done last summer."

"The oil guys usually work two or three solid weeks then have a week off. We'll make the hay when I'm home." He held onto Carson's truck, his fingers squeezing. "Isn't there a girl around that you were going to get to watch the kids? Her mother recently died?"

"Nell?"

"Yeah. Do you think she'd stay here while I'm gone?" His throat was dry, and his heart punched his ribs. He wanted to flat-out tell her that someone was staying with her because he didn't want her here alone—it was too much for her—but he didn't want to boss her. He knew he'd respond better to a suggestion than he would to an outright order. Elaine didn't seem to have a lot of rebellious tendencies, but he was trying to be courteous.

"That's to ease your mind?" she asked gently.

He'd managed to not let the commanding words come out of his mouth, but the expression on his face was probably harsher than normal.

She'd seen through everything he was trying to hide.

"My biggest struggle with this whole idea isn't the risk. If you want the possibility of a big payoff, you have to be willing to take a big risk." He ran a hand through his hair and hooked it on the back of his neck. "When I was riding, I always liked drawing the unpredictable bull. It went against typical advice and what most guys wanted. They'd want to draw the bull that would give them a solid ride. A good 80s, maybe low 90s bull. That's fine, but I always wanted the bull that had the off chance of giving me that high 90s ride. It was risky, 'cause I might end up with a low score, but the chance of coming out on top was worth it."

Carson leaned back against his chest, and he adjusted the little body into a more comfortable position.

"It's not just luck. There is that. There's always a bit of luck. But it was more because I had the confidence in my skill set, because I'd put the hard work in, because I showed up prepared." He pursed his lips. "That's the same thing here. It's not a crapshoot. I've got the contacts. We'll figure out what's going to make people beg to pay us to stay in those cabins. We'll fix them up to suit. In the meantime, we'll have our herd of cattle growing and I'll pay for everything else with a job on the oil wells."

He put the hand that wasn't holding Carson flat down on the table. "What do you say?"

She bit her lip. The stove clicked, and the wind gusted outside. He couldn't tell from the expression on her face which way she was leaning, although she continued to bite her lip, which was probably not a good sign.

Finally, she said, "I don't like the idea of you working on the oil wells."

That really wasn't what he expected to hear. He'd expected her to object to him spending all their money on a gig that might not pan out. Maybe not want to cook for a bunch of strangers.

He hadn't mentioned the extra work of cleaning the cabins. Maybe she wouldn't want all those strangers around her kids. He wasn't too keen on it himself. But he assumed the rifle that was hanging on the hooks behind the door wasn't part of her décor. He also assumed she could use it. Especially if someone were coming after her children.

Not that he wanted her to have to.

He hadn't expected her objection to the oil wells. "Why?" He couldn't argue if he didn't know her position.

She used her finger to trace the edge of the table, watching it like it was imperative that she keep her finger just so. "Please don't get offended at me."

He snorted. "Doesn't sound good."

"You limp when you don't think I'm watching. You end every day with a headache. Your back hurts when you sit too long, and when we have a storm coming, it seems like your whole body is a well of pain." Her finger stopped, and with her head still bent, she looked at him through her lashes. "It's not that I don't think you can do it, I'm just worried that you might get hurt or…killed." Her chin came up. "You can smirk at me all you want to, but it happens, you know."

He tried to get his lips to stop smiling, but he was having a rough time wrangling them into submission. He wasn't even sure why her speech made him want to grin. It made his heart glow. But she was getting annoyed. Her eyes snapped, and she moved to push away from the table.

He grabbed her wrist. He exerted no pressure. She stopped anyway.

But he couldn't keep his look serious, and she shoved back. "It's my turn to flounce out. Watch the kids."

"I did not 'flounce' out."

She yanked her coat off the hook and looked at him over her shoulder. "You flounced."

"Men don't flounce."

"Old men, who are decrepit and banged up from bull riding, flounce." She lifted a brow and yanked the door open.

"You ought to flounce more often. You look pretty dang good." He quit trying to contain his grin.

"Aargh!" The door slammed.

Rem couldn't help it. He laughed. He liked Elaine. Respected her. There was a definite attraction there, too. But this was the first time he'd thought she was downright, breathtakingly beautiful.

He laughed again, thinking of the reaction she'd have if he told her she was gorgeous when she was angry.

Chapter 14

Elaine put the last of the frosting on the cake, smoothing it out then swirling it. Her mother and sister would be here anytime. Oh, yeah. And her ex-husband. Not that she cared.

She'd already given her children the behave-or-I-will-make-you-regret-it-when-they-leave lecture, and Rem was in the shower after spending the morning moving the horse manure to a pile out behind the barn. He couldn't waste an entire Saturday on this party.

She brushed her hands down her sweater and jeans. Maybe she should have dressed up more, but she hadn't wanted anyone to think she was trying to impress James in any way. She didn't care what he thought, she really didn't, but she did hope to make her mother happy.

Yeah, she'd spent the last two days cleaning her house and the entire morning making sweet rolls, a few appetizers, and now this cake. Rem had not said a word about the grocery budget. Her mother was supposed to be bringing pizza.

She already had one pitcher of tea, the glasses, and the plates along with the silverware and a jello salad on the table.

Finishing the cake, she grabbed it, and after a second of thought, she picked up the vegetable tray in the other. A car door slamming and the crunching of snow indicated her guests had arrived as she turned to set the cake and vegetables on the table.

Her kids all came running out of the living room just as the door opened and James stepped in, not knocking, of course. This used to be his house, after all.

Banjo, who'd been sleeping at her feet on the kitchen floor, jumped up just as Elaine moved to step over him. She tried to move back, but she lost her balance and fell forward, crashing into the table. Her kitchen table, never sturdy even when it had been new thirty years ago, buckled under the awkward way she fell onto it. She lost her grip on the vegetable tray as she fell with the table to the floor.

The tea container hit her on the head, tipped over her face, lost its lid, and dumped down the front of her shirt and pants.

The crashing and banging seemed to take forever to stop as she lay in cold, wet shock.

Finally silence descended. Everything that had been on the table was now in a mess on the floor beside her. At least she still held the cake in her hand.

But Banjo, apparently wanting to apologize for their mix-up, pranced back to her, wagging his tail and licking her face. She was on her back with the slanted table behind her, and she couldn't get up with only one hand. The other hand held the cake. Banjo moved his body just in time for her to see his tail smash into the cake. She was able to keep it in her hand, but half the icing that she'd just put on it was now on Banjo's tail.

James appeared in front of her. His jaw was just as strong as it had always been, but rather than admiring it, it sent a slither of revulsion through her.

He grabbed Banjo's collar. "Gabe, get this dog and put it in our room."

"It's not 'our' room," Elaine said, knowing she sounded angry and bitter, the two things she really didn't want to be.

"Of course it's not, darling." He held his hand out. "Let me help you up."

She didn't want to take it. The idea of touching him turned her stomach. It had taken her a long, long time to come to grips with the fact that he'd left, wasn't coming back, and there wasn't anything she could do about it. Maybe somewhere, not so deep inside of her, she still felt like she was lacking something since she couldn't keep her husband. Seeing him here in front of her, knowing he was with another woman, stirred those feelings the way walking through a pond stirred the scum up.

She didn't want his help. But the tea had made everything slippery, and she was going to have a hard time getting her feet under her and standing.

She took his hand, noting the shorter fingers, the softer skin, the clamminess that Rem's didn't have. Funny how she'd never thought about it before. She shoved the inadequacy aside. He was the one who was lacking – character. He hadn't had the character to keep his vows. That was not her fault.

He pulled on her hand. Later, she was never sure whether it was her that slipped or if he yanked on her arm on purpose. However it was, when she came up, she lost her balance and slammed into James's chest, shoving him back against the kitchen counter.

"Well, we've been here all of thirty seconds, and she's already throwing herself at *my* husband." Her sister's voice, sultry, sounding like she was a two-pack-a-day smoker, slithered across the table and wound around Elaine's body, clogging her throat. Clashing with the scum that had already been stirred inside of her, making her chest burn and her neck crawl.

"Looked to me like your husband yanked my wife somewhere she didn't want to go." Rem stood in the bathroom doorway, his hair wet but combed, wearing a button-down flannel tucked into new jeans. His belt buckle glistened in the light, and he must have carried his cowboy boots into the bathroom, because he wore them as well.

The adults in the room silenced immediately. Elaine's children noticed something wasn't quite right and quieted. Some of the hotness seeped out of Elaine's chest. Maybe, if Rem were beside her, she could get through this.

"Your wife?" Elaine's mother said in a disbelieving tone.

Rem strode over to Elaine. James dropped his arms, and she stepped back. Rem reached out, sliding his hand over her cheek. "Are you okay, Chica?"

Her eyes widened a fraction at the nickname he'd never used on her before. She hadn't spoken Spanish since high school, but she thought it meant girl or maybe little girl. Not a sexy nickname, but an endearment nonetheless.

She tried to swallow and nodded, the acid burn in her chest replaced by something that felt a lot like soul balm.

"You can go change. I'll see what I can do about this mess." His thumb skimmed over her cheek. She could hardly think but knew there was something she needed to do.

Oh, that's right. Her mother.

Clearing her throat, she turned. Rem had barely touched her before this, but as she twisted, his arm slid around her waist and he pulled her against him.

She lost her train of thought again.

"Yes, ma'am. She married me just after Christmas." Rem's drawl curled in her ear, and his voice vibrated against her back.

She needed to get away from him so her brain would start functioning again.

Rem guided her around the broken table with a gentle pressure of his arm. "I'm Remington Martinez." He held his hand out. Her mother shook it. "Pleased to meet you, Mrs. Anderson."

"You're the bull rider that won the championship a year ago," her sister said.

Rem's eyes flicked to hers. He gave his chin a jerk. Then, dismissing her, he turned back to their mother.

Elaine shook herself. She should have introduced him to everyone. Not left him to figure things out on his own. "Rem, this is my sister, Corrie. And there's James. You've already figured that out, I'm sure. And their baby is Luke." She tilted her head. "I'll be back out to help you clean this up."

"Take your time, Chica," Rem murmured in a slow drawl that made her stomach do crazy things.

She stumbled a little as she walked away from him. She'd have to thank him later for coming to her defense and acting like they were truly married and not just participating in a business arrangement.

It had been a long time since she'd dressed up in anything except church clothes. She reached way back in her closet for the one western skirt she owned. She pulled it out and held it up. Made out of mesh material, it was ruffled with beads and a wide, sparkly belt. The stretchy black t-shirt she'd always worn with it was folded over the hanger. Grabbing her cowgirl boots out of the back corner, she threw everything on the bed and started changing before she lost her nerve.

She wasn't a ravishing beauty—a girl that would look good beside Rem's dark handsomeness—but at least her clothes could complement his.

The t-shirt was a little tighter over her chest than it used to be, and her stomach curved out just a little where she used to be toothpick skinny. Her boots still fit just right, though. They weren't as fancy as Rem's, but they were comfortable and felt like old friends.

Running a brush through her hair, she wished she'd taken the time to curl it. She spared another wish that she had some makeup. A little lip gloss or eyeliner at least. Her toenails were painted a sparkling coral color. Too bad no one was going to see them.

As she opened the door, she realized she should have been more concerned about the mess and that all the food had gotten ruined, rather than taking an extra thirty seconds to fix her hair and check her reflection in the glass. She was such a ninny. No one out there cared what she looked like.

The table had been righted. The pizza boxes sat on it. The second pitcher of tea had been gotten out of the refrigerator. People had found places at the table, and her children were sitting on the benches that Rem had cleaned off and brought in.

Everything was under control, and she should be happy.

But Rem was talking, and her mother was laughing with Corrie looking on. It should be good, but that's how it had started last time. Her mother and James had a great relationship, and somehow Corrie, who was her mother's favorite, ended up with her husband.

Talk about bitter and sour.

Elaine threw her shoulders back and strode into the room. Rem noticed her first. He stopped mid-sentence and stared. It was all that needed to happen for her to be happy that she'd taken the extra time to dig her skirt out.

A little grin danced around his mouth.

She gave him the sassiest smile she owned and stepped to her place at the table, sinking into her chair.

The kids had started talking, and Corrie said something, but Elaine missed it because Rem leaned over and drawled in her ear, "You're beautiful."

He didn't mean it, of course, but she appreciated the gesture.

She didn't have Corrie's nine hundred number voice, and sexy and seductive weren't really in her arsenal. But she put her tongue on her lip and leaned closer to Rem before she said in the throatiest voice she could muster, "You are definitely doing a good job of representing Texas tonight."

He cracked out a laugh.

Well, so much for being a siren. That was her sister. She was just a good cook, and once upon a time, she had a sense of humor, too. Maybe she couldn't make him look at her with longing, but she could make him laugh.

"Can we eat, now?" Gabe asked, eyeing the pizza boxes. It wasn't often that her children got a special treat like store-bought pizza.

Everyone looked to Rem at the head of the table.

"Let's pray," he said.

As Elaine bowed her head, she caught her sister's narrowed eyes, and James's annoyed look. It wasn't right to rejoice in another's suffering, but she couldn't deny it made her feel just a little good inside that James and Corrie were not sending her pitying glances tonight. That maybe, because of Rem, she had the upper hand. She had no interest in lording it over anyone, but she did love the fact that this wasn't turning out to be as hard as she'd thought it would be.

Rem had barely said "Amen" when Luke started crying.

James lifted a brow at Corrie who narrowed her eyes and jutted her chin out.

"You need to get him. I'm eating." James picked his pizza up and took a bite.

Corrie slammed her hand down on the table and shoved her chair back with a loud scrape.

"I can get him, Sweetie," their mother said, rising.

"Great," Corrie muttered, sitting back down. "He's your son, too," she said to James before turning her back on him. "So, Rem," she said in a much nicer tone, "I bet it's really hard to ride a bull."

"Yep." Rem picked up the pizza cutter and ran it across the pizza on his plate, cutting it into bite-sized pieces for Carter. "Here you go," he said to Elaine, holding out his plate with the pieces on it.

She switched him. "Thanks."

"But I heard you were really good at it." Corrie blinked her eyes, setting her chin on her hand and staring at Rem.

Elaine tried to focus on feeding Carter and eating her own food, but her heart squeezed a little.

Rem shrugged. "You know, Elaine. I was really looking forward to eating that cake. Smelled so good. But we could put candles in that last pan of sweet rolls and they would work as substitute birthday cake."

"That's a great idea. We could do that."

Corrie's bottom lip stuck out and she took a delicate bite of her pizza. The conversation seemed to flow a little better after that. Elaine appreciated that Rem had made it clear, without being rude, that Corrie wasn't getting his attention. Elaine's heart felt happy, and she wanted to thank Rem for his loyalty. She didn't, but focused on trying to be nice to set a good example for her children, not because she wanted to. But it was the right thing to do. Rem had made it a whole lot easier.

Eventually they stuck a candle in the sweet rolls, and everyone sang "Happy Birthday" to Corrie and her. They had to cut them in half so there were enough to go around, but everyone got some. It wasn't cake, but it was better than nothing.

They sat around and chatted, surprising Elaine that they could do it without snapping at each other. Again, Rem's presence helped her. Maybe time had healed her some, too. It wasn't painful to see Corrie and James together. Especially since they barely talked to each other and the few times they did, they weren't any more cordial than they were at the beginning of the meal.

It was after dark when they left. Rem went out to feed. Gabe wanted to help, so Elaine let him go while she gave the other kids baths and got them ready for bed.

She was on the couch reading a story to them when Gabe and Rem came in from the barn. Knowing that Rem was probably tired and would want to go to bed, she sent Gabe for his shower and took the kids upstairs and tucked them in. Thirty minutes later, she walked back down the stairs, thinking to slip into her room and go to bed herself.

At the bottom of the stairs, she stopped dead still and almost squealed. Rem stood in the bathroom doorway wearing a tight black t-shirt and low-slung jeans and in his bare feet.

She'd never seen his feet before, and her eyes were drawn down, for some reason.

"Hey," he said softly. Almost like he was nervous. She could hardly believe that. Rem was the most confident, borderline cocky man she knew.

She made her tongue work. "Thanks for today. That was hard for me, and you made it almost fun."

He shoved a hand in his pocket. "I liked spending the afternoon with you."

She didn't know exactly what bull riders did for fun, but she highly doubted it was anything as banal as sitting around eating pizza with a woman, her four children, and the rest of her messed-up family.

But his compliment felt sincere, even if she couldn't believe it, and she smiled.

"I'm glad you still have your skirt on." He swallowed, loud in the stillness of the kitchen.

"I just haven't had time to change." The kids seemed to take up all her time.

"Good. It's pretty, and so are you."

She closed her eyes, wishing it were true, that she were the kind of woman who belonged with a man like him. But she wasn't, and there was nothing she could do to change it.

"What's the matter?" he asked, his voice low.

She forced her lips up. "Nothing. Just tired."

"Oh." His head drooped a little, then he pushed his shoulder off the doorframe and walked slowly over. Not his usual confident stride but something more hesitant, like he didn't want to scare her away.

He stopped just a few feet away. "I didn't think I was going to like it here. The cold and the culture and people aren't what I'm used to. But I'll never get tired of watching the sun come up and go down over fields covered in snow. I love turning my face to the north wind and working through the cold."

Her heart fluttered like a leaf in a stiff breeze.

He shifted. "But what I really like is coming back in to the smell of bacon and eggs and cinnamon rolls and to see you turn around and smile at me."

She felt caught by his eyes and couldn't look away. Her hands tingled.

He took another step closer. "Dance with me?"

Her breath caught.

He set his phone on the table, and something soft and sweet started playing. Closing the last few inches between them, he put his hands on her waist.

"Was that a yes?" His voice had roughened.

Stepping into his embrace, she put her hands on his shoulders. "Yes," she said softly. "Most definitely a yes."

"Good, because I've wanted to do this for a long time, but especially since you stepped out in that skirt and those boots."

"I hope I don't step on your toe."

"A little pain will make it real."

Heat from his body pressed up and through the palms of her hands. His scent, clean and true, shimmered in the air around them. With only the light above the stove illuminating the kitchen, it felt more like a dream than reality. Although holding him, having his hands resting on the small of her back, was better than any dream she'd ever dared to dream.

They swayed gently together as the music reached a crescendo before dropping back down and fading away. Silence descended. Not an awkward one, but one that was cozy and comfortable, wrapping them in their own world.

He pulled back, just a little, and she lifted her gaze.

"I'm not sure when I started thinking about it, maybe for several weeks." His chest moved in and out.

She waited, and when he didn't say more, she prompted, "Thinking about what?"

He pressed his lips softly against her forehead. "Kiss me, Chica."

Lightly kissing down her cheek and jaw, he took advantage of her angled head and touched his mouth to the spot on her neck where her pulse surely hammered. Her fingers gripped his t-shirt, and her knees shook.

He kissed the corner of her lips, and she shivered.

"You haven't said yes," he said as close to her lips as he could get without touching.

Her hands slid off his shoulders and cupped his face. "Yes."

Rem wasn't really a go slow or sit and wait kind of guy. The fact that he had been doing both made her feel cherished, like he truly cared about her.

Her brain quit thinking when his lips touched hers. He pulled her closer, and she pressed against him willingly as the kitchen tilted and spun. Her hands slid into his hair, and in some corner of her brain that was still semi-functioning, she registered surprise that it was so soft.

He pulled away, laying his cheek on the top of her head, his chest pumping in and out. Her heart pounded, and she felt like she'd run a lap around the pasture in two feet of snow.

His hands rubbed softly over her back, but he didn't loosen his hold on her.

Finally, when her breath and heart rate had almost returned to normal, he said, "I have something for you."

A little shock went through her. "I didn't expect you to get me anything."

"It's not much. I did it a few weeks ago when I went in to Rockerton to pick up groceries and get bands." Again, he wasn't his normal confident self, like he wasn't sure what her reaction was going to be.

"What is it?"

He pulled back, and she regretted the lost contact.

Reaching into his pocket, he brought out a small box.

"Oh." Excitement thrummed though her. "A ring?"

He chuckled. "Open it."

She took it from him, their fingers brushing. She glanced up at him. His eyes were hot and settled on her.

Opening the box, she drew a breath in. "I was right. A wedding ring. But there's another ring, too." It had some type of blue stone inset in the band with diamonds on either side.

"I saw that blue, and it reminded me of your eyes. Eyes that look like the Texas sky. I don't know much about this stuff but had the thought it would be like an engagement ring." He shifted, and again she got the impression he was maybe a little nervous.

"They're beautiful. I'm kind of afraid to touch them. I don't think I've ever owned anything that nice." She put one finger out and touched the blue stone on the engagement ring. "So pretty."

"Let's see if they fit." He took the engagement ring out. "This goes on first?"

"I guess that makes sense? I don't know." She didn't want to ruin their moment by bringing up James, but he hadn't given her an engagement ring. They'd been too young and too poor to afford it.

It stuck on her knuckle then slid over and on. "Perfect," she said. "Did you get a ring for yourself?"

His lip kicked up, and she was glad his cocky smile was back. "Yeah. I guess I wanted everyone to know that I was taken."

"You're not wearing it," she said as he slipped the wedding band on. It fit just as well.

"I have it in my pocket. I wasn't sure how you were going to feel about this."

"I love it. Why wouldn't I?"

"I don't know. I mean, I know it all started as a business arrangement, but I feel like maybe that's not what I want anymore. I know it's not been very long. Just a month. And if you don't want to be more, that's fine. But I was thinking I'd like to do a little courting. We did things backward with the wedding first."

Elaine's heart had swelled so big it took up her throat and clogged her voice.

"I know money's tight, but I don't think we're so hard against it that I can't take my wife out for a nice dinner like I should have done the day we got married." He ran a finger down her cheek. "Will you go out with me, Elaine?"

For a day that she had thought would be so terrible, and had been pretty awful for a while, it had, in the last thirty minutes, become one of the best days of her life.

"I'd really like that," she said.

"We'll go Monday, then, after the kids get on the bus." His voice once again contained the confidence she was used to. "Maybe we can get Nell to watch the little ones. Would that be a hardship? To be alone with me for a day?"

"I can't think of too many things I'd rather do," she said honestly.

His head lowered, and he brushed his lips over hers. She felt the tingle clear to her toes. "Is it going to bother you if I kiss you in front of the kids?"

She shook her head lightly. She wasn't sure she had ever wanted anything more in her life than for him to kiss her.

"That's good. When I walk in that door and you turn around and smile at me, you have no idea how badly I want to feel you against me."

No, she hadn't had any idea. Not a clue.

"You can kiss me anytime," she said. Any time. All the time. Kissing Rem was a new and very pleasurable experience. One she wouldn't mind repeating as much as he wanted. He was good at it. She didn't want to think about all the girls he'd kissed to have developed the ability to make her think that she was the only one. To make her forget she had four kids and a husband who'd left her. That he'd only come to North Dakota for her ranch and money. That she was plain and boring and tired and nothing that would truly interest a man like Rem.

His lips nuzzled just below her ear. Soft and warm, they made her stomach tighten as he kept his arms around her, swaying a little like the music was still playing.

She figured she knew what he wanted. It wasn't like she was a young girl who hadn't been down this road before. It kind of surprised her that she wanted it too.

She drew back a little. His head lifted. She looked at her bedroom door then turned her head back to Rem, staring at his chin, raising her brows, putting the question in her eyes. Offering the only thing she had left that he hadn't taken when they got married.

The swaying stopped. He straightened. Her hands fell to his chest where his heart beat hard and irregular.

"I'm not gonna lie to you, Elaine. That's what I want. But it's not all I want."

She bit her lip and looked down. He'd said no. It was a nice no but still a rejection.

"Elaine?"

He waited until she raised her head and looked at him.

"What I have with you, I'm planning on having for the rest of my life." His breath huffed out on a short laugh. "Heck, an hour ago, my hands were sweating and my knees were knocking together wondering if you'd even let me kiss you."

"You've been sleeping on the couch all this time. You don't need to."

"I'm not moving into your bedroom because you feel bad for me or because you think you owe me. That's not how I want it to play out." His hands tightened on her waist, and he lowered his head once more. "Don't ask me again. A man can only be noble so long."

She was pretty sure it was disappointment that backed up in her throat. "You don't need another invitation. This one stands."

He groaned before he kissed her again. Longer and more passionately. She thought maybe he'd changed his mind, and if he came in, she wouldn't be the one doing anyone any favors. But he lifted his head and set her away.

"Happy birthday, Chica." He dropped his hands and stepped back, shoving them in his pockets. "Go to bed, lady."

Chapter 15

A snowstorm hit Sunday night. Rem had come to realize that North Dakota was like that. He could still make it to Rockerton. It might take a little longer, but he wasn't scared. He hadn't grown up driving in the snow, but it hadn't taken him long to realize that it was like most other things in life—you just needed the guts to try, a little common sense, and enough perseverance to see it through to the end.

But the kids were off school, and while he didn't mind driving in the snow, he didn't think Elaine probably wanted to white-knuckle it for four hours. Dinner with him could not be worth it.

They called Nell and let her know they weren't going.

As Rem fed that morning with Gabe, he realized he didn't have any plans for the day now that they weren't traveling. A list of things that could be done always percolated in the back of his head, and he didn't have any problem figuring out how he could spend his time.

Except he'd been looking forward to spending the day with Elaine. He'd never been this infatuated with anyone.

He liked watching her move. Loved hearing her voice. When she smiled at him, he'd do anything for her. Would do anything to keep that smile on her face.

In the back of his head, he knew it wasn't his job to make her happy, any more than anyone else controlled his happiness, but it didn't stop him from thinking about her. All day.

All night, too.

He did think maybe he'd been a little bit of a fool when he'd sent her to her room alone on Saturday night. But everything about Elaine was different than the other girls he'd known. She would stand beside him for the rest of his life. He was sure of it. It shouldn't be that hard for him to build a foundation before their relationship progressed to the physical.

Except it was. Especially when some sly part of him suggested that a physical relationship would only help strengthen any bond they already had.

He recognized it for the lie it was but couldn't say the thought didn't tempt him anyway.

"We doing the horse stalls before breakfast?" Gabe asked, sounding a lot older than his eight years and jerking Rem out of his musings.

"My stomach's telling me it's time to go in."

Gabe grinned. "Mine too."

Rem threw one last forkful of hay out the hay hole then set his fork aside. He stood for a minute looking out at the eastern sky that had exploded into shades of orange, red, and pink. It reflected off the fresh foot of snow they'd gotten overnight, and the whole world seemed to shimmer in the sub-zero air.

"That's a sight you don't see in Texas." Rem didn't even realize he was thinking that until the words were out of his mouth.

"It's pretty," Gabe said, imitating Rem's posture, his gaze flickering over the sky. Rem had noticed the boy imitated him a lot. He didn't mind, but he hadn't considered the responsibility that lay on his shoulders until that second. Gabe would pick up what he laid down. He wanted it to be good things.

He could tell him all day long what he should do. But Gabe, like most kids, would probably ignore most of the things Rem told him and simply do what he did.

Shoving those thoughts away for another day, Rem turned and ruffled the boy's hair. "What do you say we see if we can't get your mother outside to play in the snow with us for a while after breakfast?"

Gabe's eyes lit up, but then he shook his head. "She'll never do it. She always says she has too much to do. Then that someone needs to have food ready and put the baby to bed…" Gabe's voice trailed off.

"Okay. That's good to know. Let's make a plan where we take care of all her excuses before she says them."

Gabe's brows knitted together. "Huh?"

Rem allowed his cocky smile to lift up the corners of his mouth. "Like this…"

They had a deal in place by the time they walked into the house ten minutes later.

Elaine, with Carson on her hip, turned toward him with a smile on her face. He breathed deep of the scent of bacon, eggs, and cinnamon and didn't even try to stop himself from returning her smile. He did, however, toe his boots off and hang his coat up before walking over, taking Carson from her, and wrapping his free arm around her.

"Mmm. The best part of my morning," he said before he kissed her. She kissed him back just as sweetly as she had the first time, and he knew he'd be fighting that sneaky part of him that said their relationship was ready for more.

"My morning just got a lot better too," she whispered as he lifted his head. He'd never get tired of seeing her eyes glazed and her lips glisten with his kiss. Never stop wanting more. Never want less than forever.

But he stepped back. His eyes met Gabe's dancing blue ones across the table.

He cleared his throat, adjusting Carson so that the little guy's hands could reach around his neck.

"I guess you don't have anything planned for today, since we were supposed to be going to Rockerton and all."

Elaine was flipping the eggs carefully so she didn't break the yolks and didn't look up. "I always have things I could be doing. I'm sure you know what I mean."

Gabe's face fell, but it still held out hope that Rem would prevail.

"I don't suppose you have a package of hot dogs in the fridge?" Rem affected his best innocent air as he bounced Carson up and down before flying him into his high chair.

"I do." She looked up. "Why?"

"Do we have marshmallows?" He answered her question with one of his own.

"I think I have a bag in the cupboard."

"What about graham crackers?"

Understanding crept across her face. She looked over her shoulder and laughed outright, shaking her spatula at Rem. "You've got the innocent act down, but your partner in crime looks as guilty as a bank robber holding a bucket of cash."

Rem gave her his best good ol' boy smile. "So was that a yes to the graham cracker question?"

She laughed again, shaking her head and turning back to the stove. "I do have graham crackers, actually, and—" She carefully lifted the eggs out and flipped them over onto a plate. "I also have four chocolate bars. I bought them for the kids for Valentine's Day the last time we were in town."

"So I can borrow them?"

"Borrow?" She lifted a brow, stopping with the plate in her hand.

"Sure. Next time we go into town, I'll replace them. Maybe they'll multiply."

"Chocolate bars do not reproduce."

He took the plate from her. "I didn't say reproduce. I said multiply. You're talking science. I'm talking math. No wonder they say men are from Mars and women are from somewhere a lot weirder and farther away."

"If you want my chocolate bars, you'd better be nice to me." She put a hand on her hip.

"How about I feed your cows for you? Oh, wait. I already did that."

"*My* cows? They're my cows?"

"Sure. When they're hungry, they're yours."

"Oh." She grunted. "I suppose they're your cows when we're loading them on the trailer and taking them to the slaughterhouse."

"Tell you what, you can keep them until they're unloaded, then they're mine," he said smugly.

She rolled her eyes. "Wow, you're so generous."

"Mr. Rem." Gabe pulled his face into a "what are you doing" look.

"So, Elaine," Rem cleared his throat. "You know how you're always doing that family night and everything?"

"Yeah?"

"I think, since we already don't have anything planned, we should just have a family day."

"That's a great idea."

"I think we should do it outside."

She stopped with her butt halfway to the chair. "Outside?"

"Sure. I've got some skids that need to be burned anyway. So we'll have a fire. We have hot dogs and can make s'mores. I've never been ice fishing, but there's some fishing stuff in the barn. We can pack it all up and head to the lake."

"I think that last statement is something people say in the summer."

"But this is North Dakota. We're not really like the rest of the country. We do things our own way here."

"We?" She laughed.

"I became an honorary native when I married you."

"I don't think it works that way here. It's merit based."

"If I bring our cows through the winter without losing any, is that good enough?"

"Fifty winters, maybe."

"Wow. High standards."

"I think you can meet them."

"Sure can."

"So you want to take Gabe and go to the lake?"

"Oh, Chica, you misunderstood."

"I did?"

"I want you, and all of the kids, to go to the lake with me."

Elaine pressed her lips together.

"Come on, Mom. You never play with us outside."

"Outside is a lot different than packing everything up and going to the lake. We only have one snowmobile, and it would take at least four trips, maybe more, 'til we got all the food, and we should take dry clothes, plus you'd have to take all that wood for a fire…"

"We could just stay here and play outside," Gabe wheedled.

"I think that would be much better."

"If we don't go to the lake, you'll come out?"

"Yes," she said with a decisive nod of her head.

"Yes!" Gabe jumped up, fist pumping the air. He skipped around to Rem and threw his arms around his neck. "You were right. It worked."

"Shh." Rem put his finger over his lips, but it was too late.

"I've been duped!" Elaine exclaimed. "You guys did that on purpose."

"It was Mr. Rem's idea. He said aim high, and then you can settle for what you really want. He was right. You agreed to come outside and play with us."

"Can we really have a bonfire?" Heaven asked. "And roast hot dogs and marshmallows?"

All the kids, even Carson, who probably didn't understand what was going on, looked at their mother. Rem knew Elaine was lost. No one could resist all those sweet little eyes.

But just to sweeten the pot, he said, "We'll cook dinner so you don't have to, and you can have a nap this afternoon."

"Oh, you said the 'n' word. I like it."

Rem looked around the table. "That was a yes, guys."

~~~

Elaine couldn't believe that they'd talked her into going outside. When was the last time she'd played in the snow with her kids? Before James left, for sure. She just didn't have the energy to do all the essential tasks plus take on more.

But Rem stuffed Carson in his snowsuit, which was a job and a half, and got his boots and hat on. Carson's face was red with excitement by the time they made it out the door.

The temperature had come up to the mid-twenties, so she didn't worry about the kids getting too cold. Even Carson should be fine in temperatures that warm.

Rem started the fire with the old skids then helped them build a snow fort. They only built one, overlooking the driveway so they could attack anyone who attempted to come up with nefarious intentions.

Elaine didn't bother to point out that such a person probably would not use the driveway to get there, and not in the middle of the day; she didn't want to be a wet blanket when the kids were having so much fun.

She was huddled in the snow fort with Carson, stockpiling ammunition, which consisted of snowballs, when Gabe and Heaven launched a sneak attack on Rem as he gathered more snow to bring back to the fort.

His deep laugh carried over the yard as he ran, pitching over the wall of the fort headfirst and landing beside Carson and her on his stomach, his boots sticking over the top of the wall.

He was laughing, his face against the snowy floor, before he pushed himself up and peeked over the wall.

The kids were waiting. Heaven didn't have as strong a throwing arm as Gabe, but she didn't miss.

Rem ducked back down, laughing even harder, with snow covering his eyes, nose, and mouth.

He pulled enough of it off to say, "If you're gonna peek over the wall, you should do it with your mouth shut."

"Snow forts 101," she said with a cheeky grin.

"You could have mentioned that thirty seconds ago."

"You want to be a native, there're some things you just have to learn the hard way." She grabbed a couple of snowballs. "I'll create a diversion. Then you can peek over."

By the time they had played and roasted hot dogs and made s'mores, they were all tired but happy and glowing.

Her kids were almost dead on their feet as they tramped through the door. "I do believe Rem said naps after playing."

She barely got a complaint with that statement, so they took their snow clothes off and threw them in the dryer, and she helped Elijah and Carson get dry things on while Heaven and Gabe got themselves changed.

"You two can read if you don't want to nap, but I think a rest will do us all good." Elaine looked at the bright red and happy faces of her children and felt a rush of gratitude in her chest for Rem insisting that she needed to take some time off and play.

He'd been right.

She was pretty sure Carson was asleep before she even stepped out of his room. She could use a good nap herself, although she didn't have anything started for supper.

But when she walked into the kitchen, there was already a package of hamburger sitting on the counter, thawing along with a bag of rolls. A package of frozen corn sat in a pot on the stove, ready to cook.

She was going to get a nap after all, but she needed to thank Rem first. Sticking her head in the doorway of the living room, she saw Rem lying on the couch, far against the back. His eyes were open, like he'd been waiting for her.

"Thanks," she said, softly but heartfelt.

"Take a nap with me," he said, his voice coming out with the extra drawl it had when he was nervous. It was his tell. One sure couldn't look at him and know that he was anything but completely confident.

She probably had a tell, too. Whatever it was, it had to be going strong.

Her stomach flipped, but she tried to match his casual attitude.

"You think we'll both fit?" He was a big man.

"You're asking if I'm gonna let you fall off, aren't you? Kinda hurt my feelings."

She snorted and walked over, sitting down carefully before stretching out beside him. His arm came around her immediately, pulling her in to his hard warmth. He buried his nose in her hair and breathed deep.

"Thanks for not getting mad at me for engaging in a little trickery."

"I'm glad you did. I had a lot of fun, and the kids had a blast."

"I had fun too," he said, his voice coming low and soft. "Seems like I can do anything with you and have a good time."

"Really? And here I thought it was the s'mores that made your day."

"It takes patience to roast a marshmallow until the center is gooey. You make them perfect every time. Pretty much the way everything you cook comes out perfectly."

"When you do it as much as I do…"

"You don't enjoy it?" He seemed upset at the thought.

"I do." She snuggled deeper into the couch, tucking her legs between his, feeling warm and sleepy. "It's fun to cook. I think it's almost as much fun to watch people enjoy what I cook."

"Then you must love watching me."

Her eyes drifted shut. "I do. You're a beautiful man, Rem."

Chapter 16

Rem kind of expected winter to fade away by the end of February. It didn't. It was still going pretty strong in March, too.

On March 14th, he called his mother to wish her a happy birthday. Elaine had gone in to the school since it was her day to be the classroom mother in Heaven's class. Rem had the two little boys, although they were both sleeping when he called his mother.

"Hello?"

"Hey, Mom. Happy birthday."

"Remington, you haven't called since Christmas."

There'd been plenty of times when he'd been out on the circuit where he'd gone longer than three months without talking to his folks, but he supposed they watched him on TV and knew he was still upright.

"Sorry. I've been busy." That was true. He had the tractor back together and running well. He'd also taken the round baler apart and refurbished it. It had needed it.

Not to mention they'd sold his cattle and bought new. They would arrive in another month.

"Too busy to take a minute to call your mother. That's sad."

"How've you been?" It *was* sad. He'd not thought of it before, but he tried to picture Elaine and how she'd feel if her boys left and only called a couple of times a year. She probably wouldn't say anything, but she'd be hurt.

"We've been just fine. Your dad was talking about you the other day. He's got some things he wants to discuss with you."

"He knows my number."

"Don't be like that, Rem."

"I'm not. I'm over it all."

"Rem, I understand what happened and what Olivia did was hard. I don't expect you to just get over it. But this thing with your dad…you know he gets angry then he lets it go."

Texas temper. That's what his mom always called it. "It's fine, Mom."

"If it's fine, why are you still gone?"

Rem ran a hand through his hair then braced it against the doorjamb. He'd never actually dropped a bomb on anyone, but he wondered if this suspended-in-space feeling was how one felt before they pushed the button to launch the missile.

"I got married."

Shocked silence preceded the eruption he was expecting.

"You got married? Seriously, Rem? You couldn't tell your family, your *mother*, that you were even engaged? Just 'I got married'? We weren't invited to the wedding? And who is this girl? She must not be someone we'd approve of if you didn't bother to tell us. When did this happen anyway?"

He waited until she clamped her mouth shut with an audible sound he could hear over the phone.

"I married her the day after Christmas."

"You've been married for *three months* and are just now telling me? This is outrageous. I cannot believe you could have grown up in my home and still be so calloused and inconsiderate. Did it not occur to you that this is something your mother and the rest of your family would like to know?"

"I'm telling you now."

"Did you just marry her to get back at your brother and Olivia?"

"No."

Her voice softened. "You heard that Max and Olivia split up?"

His brother hadn't even lasted a year with her. Didn't surprise him. He'd wasted far too much time on Olivia. If he'd had any idea that there was a woman like Elaine in the world, he wouldn't have given Olivia the time of day. Although maybe he'd been too immature to appreciate a woman like Elaine until he'd gone through what he had with Olivia.

That didn't paint him in the best light, but it was probably pretty close to the truth.

"No. That's too bad." He couldn't find it in himself to be happy about their split. If it hadn't been for Max and Olivia and what they did, he wouldn't have found Elaine.

"Where are you?"

"North Dakota."

The line went so quiet he thought the connection might have been lost.

"Where?" she asked.

He was unsure if she truly hadn't heard or just couldn't believe it.

"North Dakota. It's just south of Canada. That's the country that borders the US to—"

"I know where Canada is," his mother snapped. "I don't appreciate the disrespect."

"It's beautiful here, Mom. You wouldn't believe it."

He could almost picture her rolling her eyes. His mother was a seventh-generation Texan, and it was almost a sacrilege to suggest there was any place on earth better than Texas. He'd be better off taking the Lord's name in vain than telling her he loved North Dakota.

"You said you're not holding a grudge against your dad or your brother."

"I'm not."

"And it's just coincidence that we haven't heard from you in three months."

"I told you I've been busy."

"Then buy a plane ticket and come down and visit." There was a deliberate pause. He understood what it meant. "Bring your wife." She said "wife" like she was holding her nose.

"I don't think I'm going to have time this year." He could swing the time. No problem. But the kids definitely couldn't go. And he thought it might be hard for Elaine to leave them for at least three days. They might be able to squeeze a trip to Texas into two, but it would be tough.

"Remington." His mother used the voice that brooked no argument when he was a child. "Your dad has pancreatic cancer. There's a five percent survival rate. You need to come down."

Shock waves punched up his neck, making him dizzy. His hand gripped the doorjamb tighter, while his fingers curled around his phone. His eyes tunneled. He couldn't let his dad die with their last fight between them.

"I'll be down."

~~~

That night after the kids went to bed, Elaine walked soundlessly down the stairs. Rem stood at his normal spot, with his shoulder leaning against the bathroom doorjamb, in t-shirt and jeans, bare feet. His hair was wet, and his hands were in his pockets.

Normally when she came down, his eyes were hot and followed her every move. Most nights, he played a few songs on his phone and they danced in the kitchen together. Maybe they'd talk some, maybe they wouldn't. There was definitely kissing involved. Then he'd head to the living room, and she'd close her bedroom door behind her.

But tonight, his eyes were pointed to the ground, and he seemed lost in thought. He'd been quiet all evening, but she hadn't really noticed until just now. Sometimes the kids took up all of her attention.

He looked up. "I should help you with them."

"It works out well that you shower while I put them to bed."

He didn't move across the floor like he usually did. Fear curled in the pit of her stomach. He'd been so kind and considerate the last few months. He'd worked hard outside and seemed to have fun with the kids. She thought he might actually like it here.

But what if he didn't?

She gave her head a shake, unwilling to allow herself to think like that. He'd said he was staying, and so far, he'd done everything he'd said he was going to do. He'd not lied. Not to her. Not to the kids.

He hadn't done anything to deserve her lack of faith.

But it took more courage than she'd like to admit for her to force her feet to move across the floor. She stopped in front of him, pressing herself against him and leaning her head on his chest.

"You want to tell me about it?" she asked, wishing her voice didn't sound as timid as she felt.

"Today was my mother's birthday. I called her." His hands came up, and he pulled her even more tightly against him. "My dad has cancer, and his chances of surviving it are not good."

Ah, yes. Elaine's original fear multiplied and spread up into her chest, causing her heart to skitter and shake and her breathing to be shallow and fast.

She pulled on every ounce of unselfishness she possessed and prayed her voice would be steady and clear. "Then you should go see him."

"I want to." She could hear just how much in his voice. His chest expanded and he blew a breath out. "I want you to come with me."

Elaine closed her eyes. Her arms tightened around him. "What about the children?"

"Would Nell be able to watch them for a couple of days?"

"I can ask." They would be fine with Nell, although Elaine had never left them other than to go to the hospital to have each of them. Even then, she'd never stayed in the hospital long.

"I'd like to leave tomorrow if we can. The next day at the latest."

"What about the stock?"

"Ford will help me. If he can't, there's a couple of people from church that will. It's not rocket science, it's just time."

"I'll call Nell first thing in the morning."

"Thanks."

~~~

Nell was able to come and showed up the next day before the kids got home from school. Rem was out doing the evening feeding early.

Elaine opened the door, and Nell blew in. "My goodness, the wind is strong." Her face, rosy-cheeked with sparkling eyes, held a smile.

"I'm so glad you could do this on short notice."

"Not a problem," Nell said, although something in her eyes made Elaine wonder if maybe Nell actually did have a problem getting out of her house.

Her mother had died before Christmas. Elaine thought that might be the only thing keeping her living at her home with her stepfather and two stepsisters, but it had been over three months, and Nell was still there.

"Were the roads okay?" With the strong wind, there were bound to be some drifts. Normally Nell walked across the fields to their house. It was only about three miles, but as deep as the snow was right now, it would be a hard walk.

"My stepdad let me use his old Ford." She took her hat off, and her short blond hair stuck up all over the place from the static. "But I had a flat tire on the way here."

"Oh, no. That's awful. With this wind, I bet changing it was tough."

"It probably was." She tilted her head. "I've never had this happen before. But as I was stopped, this sports car—it was probably one of those expensive things because it wasn't a brand I recognized—pulled up beside me. We're on the interstate, you know. It wasn't terribly busy, but there were still trucks whizzing by and everything."

She noticed the pan of potatoes on the counter that Elaine hadn't pared yet and walked over, grabbing a knife and starting to pare them.

"Anyway, this guy in a fancy suit gets out. I don't know what an expensive suit looks like, but this isn't anything you can get at Walmart."

Elaine tilted her head, her brow furrowed. "Walmart doesn't have suits."

"If they did, they wouldn't look like this. I bet that thing cost a thousand bucks. Or more." Nell grunted. "And shoes. Man, his shoes. I've never seen shoes like that. Shiny and just *rich*. Like really rich."

"Doesn't sound to me like a man like that would stop, let alone be able to help."

"That's the really strange thing. He did. He changed the tire. In that suit and those shoes. His fingernails were perfect." She held her hands out. "Look at my hands. It's like I have the man hands, and he had the woman hands, except he got the tools out, and he knew how to use them."

"Did he wear gloves?"

"No! Isn't that crazy? He *must* be from North Dakota. If you're not used to this cold, you just can't take it like that. But this guy did."

"Oh? He was young?"

"Thirties. Maybe." She shrugged. "Sometimes this country ages you quick. But I don't think he's had a rough life."

"Not if his hands are any indication."

"Exactly. Oh." Nell set her knife down and went over to her coat. "He gave me this." She pulled a brochure out of her coat's pocket and handed it to Elaine. "He said I should go."

Elaine took the brochure. "A ball? Who even has balls anymore? That's weird."

"Yeah. You know those stories you hear about people who meet angels or even dead people along the road in a storm, and the angels or whatever help them out, then the people find out later that someone who looked just like the person who helped them died on that stretch of road?"

"I guess," Elaine said, a little unsure. It sounded like hocus-pocus stuff that she stayed away from.

"This feels so much like that. I mean, he wasn't slipping in the snow, even though he had those fancy shoes on. His car definitely wasn't the kind of car that someone could drive on our roads and not get stuck. And he didn't seem to be from around here, but he didn't get cold. Especially his hands."

"That is weird." Elaine scanned over the brochure. "This ball is supposed to be held on May 1st at the Sweet Water Ranch. I haven't heard anything about it."

"He said that I was the first one to get a brochure." Nell's eyes were a little dreamy, and Elaine suspected there were a few things she wasn't being told. "He told me he really wanted me to go."

"Then you should go."

Nell snorted. "My stepdad will never let me borrow a vehicle to drive to a party just to have fun. Plus," she pointed at the brochure, "see this? It says 'formal.' Elaine, this is the most formal thing I own." She stepped back from the sink and ran her hands up and down her jeans and old, long-sleeved t-shirt and puffer vest.

Nell pulled the brochure back. "But look here." She pointed to the fine print at the bottom. "It says 'Maids and servers will be needed. Apply online. Pay will be $500 for the day.'" Nell's face practically glowed. "I could do that! I'm great at cleaning, and I can be very polite."

Elaine laughed. "Those are the only qualifications?"

"It doesn't say, but I'm going to apply."

"If you need a reference, you can put me down. I think sometimes my kids love you more than they love me. And I know my house is always cleaner when you leave."

"I'll do that. Thanks." Nell rinsed a potato off and cut it into pieces over the pot Elaine had on the stove.

The kids were in good hands, Elaine assured herself. And everything would be fine.

Chapter 17

Rem pulled the rented car into the familiar ranch driveway.

Elaine had never flown before, never even been out of North Dakota, she admitted to him once the plane had taken off. She'd enjoyed the flight, and he'd enjoyed watching her. It looked like she liked Texas, too. Her eyes were big, and it was almost like she was trying to look everywhere at once, despite how tired she must be.

They'd slept some at the Dallas airport while waiting for their connecting flight early this morning, and she'd slept a little on the plane. But she still had black circles under her eyes.

Not as careworn as she'd looked when he'd first met her. He liked to think that maybe he had something to do with that. Maybe they didn't get their billion dollars, but he'd shouldered a lot of her worries, leaving her free to be a wife and mother. She was still involved in the ranch, of course, but the problems and work didn't weigh her down.

"There's our house." He nodded at the brown, one-story home. The green roof set it off, and the wide porch was screened in. The barn was not much farther on. He recognized the bull in the corral. One his brother had bought. Prince Charming. Rem wouldn't have wasted the money.

Max had bought him, thinking to do what Rem had been doing—raising high-dollar bucking bulls. It was a risk, no doubt. Prince Charming was a high-dollar dud.

But he was a pretty bull, bluish gray over his back that dappled down to dusty white on his belly and legs. He'd never see the inside of a professional bull riding chute, but worst of all, he had a tendency to throw sons who were even more worthless than he was.

Max had made a mistake. Unfortunately it only seemed to make him resent Rem more. Maybe because Rem's bulls had been showing some promise before he sold them.

It was a bit of a shock getting off the airplane and not seeing white snow everywhere. Now, seeing the brown and green Texas Hill Country landscape, it made him wonder what Elaine's and his ranch would look like when spring finally came to North Dakota.

He parked at the rail, just as his mother came out the screened porch, followed by two puffy white dogs. Salt and Sugar. He'd been out on tour when she'd gotten them and didn't know them that well, but they seemed nice. Definitely smaller and less energetic than Banjo.

"It's beautiful." Elaine finally broke her silence.

"Spring is the best time of year in Texas."

She laughed. "It won't be spring until next week."

"The next week, it's summer." He grinned over at her, glad she seemed okay. If his mother hadn't been striding toward them, he'd have made a joke about North Dakota and its seemingly endless winter, but he saved it for another time.

"That's my mom. Come on, I'll introduce you." He got out, walking around to open Elaine's door. She was already out, so he just closed it and took her hand.

His mother, tall and slim, met them at the front of their car. "Rem!" she exclaimed, holding out her arms and wrapping them around him. She smelled like sandalwood and some kind of expensive perfume. Familiar but not a scent he'd missed.

He put his free arm around her, squeezing a little but keeping a hold of Elaine's hand. His mom could be a little overwhelming, and Elaine wasn't pushy enough to stand her ground.

Finally she pulled back, looking him up and down like she was making sure he hadn't grown a second head.

"You're more pale than I've ever seen you. Are you feeling okay?"

"Just fine, Mom." He pulled Elaine to his side and dropped her hand so he could put his arm around her. "This is my wife, Elaine."

His mom looked at Elaine for the first time. "My goodness, you're as white as a sheet."

Elaine's mouth held a half-smile, like she wasn't sure what kind of reaction to give to a statement like that.

Rem didn't know either. "It's winter in North Dakota. We're not out in the sun much this time of year."

"We? Like you're a North Dakotan?"

He didn't want to start an argument, so he bit his tongue rather than give the answer that wanted to slip out.

"You have a beautiful place here, Mrs. Martinez." Elaine's voice was sincere.

"Thank you, sweetie. It takes a lot of work to keep this place up. I don't know if Rem told you or not, but his dad is sick, and we could really use his help." His mother's tone was only a little condescending; probably she was still mad because he hadn't told her he was married. He didn't want Elaine to have to pay for that.

But a more immediate issue had arisen. Rem had noticed that the grass was a little high, weeds were growing in places where they'd never allowed weeds to grow before, and being that it was spring, there should be cows in the near pasture so they could keep an eye on them before they freshened. But there weren't.

Was the ranch in trouble?

"Where's Dad?"

"He's sleeping. The treatments really take a toll on him."

"Max?"

His mother drew in a breath and pushed it back out. "He's taken Olivia's leaving pretty hard."

Rem studied her. Back when they were younger, he'd been the one with the drinking problem. It had taken two stints in jail and a determination to focus on a championship for him to overcome his issues.

Max, on the other hand, had always been a casual drinker. Something like this might have pushed him past the socially acceptable point and into a problem area.

"In what way?" he asked cautiously.

"He's depressed, of course." His mother tilted her head, tugging her shirt down, before she said, "You remember Cord Wingate? His dad was president of the First National Bank of Texas?"

"Yeah?"

"Well, she…ran off with him."

"You're kidding. They haven't even been married a year."

She lifted a shoulder in a graceful shrug. "Cord bought the Triple D hunting camp that's about forty-five minutes south of here. Six point two million dollars. I think that was looking a little better than this, with all the work there is to do here."

"You need to hire some people."

"You know how your dad is. He wants to do everything himself. Except now he can't, so he's pushing Max to do it all. Max can't take the pressure."

Elaine's arm slipped around his waist, and he realized they were still standing in the yard. His mother hadn't invited him in.

"I assumed we'd stay here tonight?"

"Oh, yes. Of course." His mother put a hand on her head and gave it a little shake. Her auburn hair stayed firmly in place. "I'm sorry. Please, come in. I have your old room ready. I assumed you'd want to see your dad then maybe ride around the ranch some?"

He walked around and pulled their bags from the trunk. "I don't know. We've been up most of the night. I'm tired, and Elaine probably is too." He looked down at her. She didn't have to tell him she was tired; he could see it in the tightness of her eyes and the drooping of her shoulders. She leaned against him as they walked.

"Oh, really?" His mother's green eyes flashed to Elaine. Her mouth tightened like she disapproved. "You're not going to be here long. I thought for sure you'd want to see everything."

"We're here because Dad's sick and I want to see him. You also said he wanted to talk to me." Rem opened the door for his mother. He met Elaine's eyes as she went through. Elaine wasn't getting the best of welcomes here, but she didn't seem upset. Not like he was. He knew his mother was angry that he married without her knowledge and without her knowing his bride, but it was wrong for her to be punishing Elaine.

The house was cool as they stepped in and removed their shoes. The tile floor was even cooler through his socks. He marveled at the differences. In Texas, everything was about keeping them cool and comfortable. In North Dakota, they were always trying to stay warm.

Compared to the house they lived in, his old home felt like a mansion, with high ceilings and large rooms all decorated in earthy colors. It was wide and spacious; he'd forgotten how much he loved this house.

"You know where your room is." His mother broke into his thoughts. "If you want to ride around the ranch, you know you're welcome. I have a nice meal planned for tonight with a few old friends. I told people to come around seven. Reeva is getting the back barbeque pit area ready, and our chef has a brisket in the smoker."

"Will you text me when Dad wakes up?"

"I will. I know he'll want to see you."

"Thanks." He pulled on Elaine's hand and led her past the large kitchen with the big bar that seated ten people, through the living room with comfortable couches and greenery and artwork placed in strategic locations, and down the hallway to his old room on the right.

They stepped into the oversized room. The comforter on the large wooden bed was new. But the bed itself, along with the two matching dressers, was the same as he'd grown up with. The door was open to the master bath where there was a whirlpool tub and a stand-up shower. The shades were open. His windows overlooked the hill country to the south. It was a view he'd loved all his life.

Walking into his room felt like coming home in a way his mother's arms had not. He turned to Elaine. "How are you holding up?"

"I'm fine."

He figured that's what she'd say.

He tried a different tact. "You want to ride and see the ranch? Or do you want to rest?"

She swallowed and looked at the bed. He hadn't considered that they'd be sharing one tonight. Although she seemed comfortable with him and they had a solid friendship, he'd not suggested moving into her room, and she hadn't made the offer again. It was going to happen eventually, sooner rather than later, probably, but he didn't want her to have any regrets. Going too fast might be a problem, but going too slow wouldn't hurt anything.

"I can sleep on the floor if that makes you uncomfortable."

Her eyes widened. "Oh, no." Her cheeks reddened. "I wasn't thinking about that. I was just considering, I'll be fine if we see the ranch, and I really want to." She stepped closer to him and ran her hands up his chest. Yeah, she was definitely comfortable with him. "This is where you grew up, and you love it. I want to love it, too."

His hands slid over her back and pulled her closer. "I love it, that's true. I guess I'd forgotten how much until we drove up today. But there's a ranch in North Dakota that has stolen my heart."

She reached up and kissed the bottom of his jaw. "Show me your ranch, Rem."

His eyes closed, and his hands tightened on her back before he let her go. "Come on, you're gonna love it."

Chapter 18

When Rem said "ride," he'd meant horses. Elaine had never ridden a horse in her life. Because of James, they kept three for the children. Elaine could brush them, clean their stalls, and even clean their hooves, but she'd never been on their backs.

She'd been terrified and trying to hide it, although she'd always heard a horse could tell. Either her horse was a little slow on the uptake, or she was a good faker. Whichever it was, she'd managed to ride beside Rem without falling off or having a panic attack.

Rem had probably noticed her discomfort more than the horse. He constantly amazed her by how he seemed to know what she was thinking and feeling. In this case, he'd kept the horses to a walk. Maybe that was the normal speed at which they rode.

Regardless, she'd been grateful, since she had no idea how to get her horse to go faster or, more importantly in her opinion, how to steer it or get it to stop. Thankfully it was happy to plod along beside Rem's mount. Meanwhile, Rem never mentioned her inadequacy, and she had a great time, listening to Rem brag about his home and the state he loved.

Still, she was pretty happy to get off the horse. She was also sore. Muscles that she hadn't even known she had twinged in painful chorus as she pulled the saddle off her horse.

Rem's phone buzzed as they walked into the house.

"Mom says Dad is awake. You mind getting a shower while I run in and talk to him quickly?" Rem asked, holding the door open for her.

"Not at all," she answered, wondering if she might not even meet his dad.

"Can you find your way to our room?"

"Sure." The house was big but not twisty, and she could easily find it.

He pulled her close and kissed her hard and fast. "Thanks, Chica."

She was a little dazed as he pulled away and strode in the opposite direction. She stood and blinked, a bemused smile on her face. That kiss could have lasted a little longer.

"Hey, sister."

Elaine jerked around, her eyes searching frantically around the kitchen then the living room for the source of the lazy drawl and the words that were slightly slurred.

Finally she saw the man slouched on the easy chair in the corner of the living room. She walked slowly closer, thinking this must be Max as there were definitely similarities between him and Rem.

Rem didn't hate him. He almost seemed sad when he talked about Max.

"Hello," she said. "I'm Elaine."

"I know who you are." The man didn't move, but his eyes, dark brown where Rem's were black, followed her.

"Then you know I'm Rem's wife."

The man snorted. "Rem always lands on his feet. Women or bulls, doesn't matter. Gets bucked off, lands on his feet." His hand came down, smacking on his lap as though to emphasize his point.

"Has it occurred to you that perhaps Rem works hard and isn't afraid to go after what he wants, even if it involves sacrifices, and maybe that's why he's successful?" Elaine laid her hand on the back of the couch, staying a good eight feet away from the man, for all that he seemed to be sloshed but mostly harmless.

"No," he said flatly. "It hasn't."

Elaine snorted. "Then maybe it should. Because that's the truth. Hard work trumps talent any day of the week. Rem sees what he wants, then he works to get it."

"He's got you brainwashed."

"I'm just telling you what I've seen."

"Pretty sure Rem didn't know any chicks in the Dakotas. You probably haven't even known him for a year. Half a year, maybe. I'm his brother. I grew up with him." The man got a sly look on his face. "You know last year this time, Rem's fiancée was pregnant."

As much as she didn't want the man to get a reaction from her, Elaine gasped.

"You can finish that story, Max." Rem arrived at her side on stocking feet. She hadn't heard him come.

"I'll let you tell it, bro. I'm sure your version is better than mine."

"I had a drinking problem at one time, Max, as you well know. If you want to talk about it, I'm here." Rem took Elaine's hand. The slide of his calloused fingers through hers soothed her like it always did. "You mind coming? My dad wants to meet you."

"Of course," she said as she followed him, hoping she'd hear the rest of the fiancée story. That hadn't been in the report she'd read. Did Rem have a baby somewhere? He'd not mentioned it at all.

She put a hand over her stomach. The idea of Rem having a child was shocking, but she could handle that. It was more the thought that he'd kept the information from her that really upset her.

"What a great son you are, Rem. You know he's going to give you the ranch. You don't have to suck up anymore." Max's words were even more slurred as his anger rose.

Elaine waited for Rem to tell Max that he wasn't taking the ranch. That Max was welcome to it because he had his own spread up north, but he didn't, and her heart sank a little. Rem walked away without answering.

It was obvious when they reached the sickroom that Rem had been wise in not delaying the trip to see his dad.

Sunken features, inability to lift his head off the pillow, and it even seemed like he could barely open his eyes. Oxygen hissed from a canister beside him, and there were deep grooves between his eyes like he was in pain even while he slept.

"Dad?" Rem said softly.

The man's eyes slowly opened. Elaine could see where Rem got his midnight black hair and eyes. And his height, as his feet reached to the end of the bed.

"Remington," the man said weakly.

"This is my wife, Elaine."

His eyes, barely open, moved past Rem and landed on her. Despite his weakness, he still had what seemed like a commanding presence. Or maybe that was just Rem, giving him deference.

"Elaine. That's a good Texan name." The man's voice was gruff although soft. Elaine imagined it had probably been a booming voice back when his health was good.

"Thanks," she said.

"Come a little closer, girl."

She moved forward, to his bedside, while he peered up at her.

"She's too soft for you, son." The man coughed. "She looks like an angel with all that white hair."

"She's not soft, Dad, but she is an angel." Rem's hand landed on her shoulder.

His dad wheezed. "You need a strong woman that'll work beside you. Not a soft one that you have to carry along with everything else."

"Elaine is perfect for me, Dad."

"When you're running this ranch, she'll be a liability."

Elaine expected Rem to gently correct his dad—they were not moving to Texas—but he didn't.

"Elaine is as strong as any woman I've ever met."

His dad coughed then lowered his bushy brows over eyes that were filled with pain but still sharp. "She's standing there like a church mouse, letting us talk about her."

"Strong doesn't equal loud. Or pushy. It's not about who can throw the loudest fit."

His dad didn't argue with him.

"Did you ever think that maybe it takes more strength to deny yourself and give up what you want for someone else's benefit than it does to demand that you get it for yourself?" Rem's hand tightened on her shoulder.

His dad looked away. "There's some truth to that."

"Of course there is. The strongest person in the room is usually not the loudest or the most pushy. It's the one that's still doing right when everyone else has quit. That's Elaine, Dad."

Rem's words warmed her to her very toes, but they also started an ache between her shoulder blades. Did he really mean that? Or was that his way of preparing her to have to give up her home in North Dakota and travel to Texas to live here?

Part of the reason she'd held on so fiercely to her ranch was because it had been in her family for so long. That was the point of marrying a total stranger—to save it. Rem had come up with a good plan, they'd gotten someone in to do the work that needed to be done on the cabins, work that was almost finished, and Rem's friends who owned the vacation booking service had said that there'd been a lot of interest in the cabins.

Everything that they'd been working toward was coming around. Was he going to leave it all and go to Texas? Was he going to expect her to come too? Or, as she feared, was he going to leave her in North Dakota and move south by himself?

Rem said good night to his dad and pulled her out of the room. She followed silently beside him, trying to reassure herself that nothing Rem had ever done had indicated that he didn't intend to keep his word. She needed to trust him.

It was hard. After what James had done, people probably couldn't blame her for struggling with trust, but no one was going to look at Rem and confuse him with James.

She needed to shove her doubts aside.

Max was no longer on the couch as they passed through. Rem's head turned to look. His hand tightened just a bit on hers, so she knew Max stressed him in some way. Whether it was because Max had been willing to take his fiancée from him, or whether it was concern for Max, she wasn't sure.

"You've been quiet," he said as he opened the door to his room and waited for her to pass through.

"I guess I'm tired."

He'd never let go of her hand, and once he shut the door, he pulled her to him. "Talk to me, Elaine."

She lifted her head. "What happened to the baby your fiancée was carrying?"

A shock passed though Rem's body like he couldn't believe she would ask something like that. Or maybe he didn't like thinking about it.

His jaw tightened. He seemed angry, but she didn't think the anger was directed at her. "I wanted to move the wedding up. She didn't." He lifted a shoulder, but Elaine wasn't fooled into thinking it didn't matter to him. "She had an abortion. She paid for it with my money."

Elaine gasped softly.

Rem's eyes flashed. "That betrayal was worse than when she left me a month later to be with Max."

She held him for a minute, knowing there was nothing she could say. In a way, she knew that if Olivia hadn't done what she did, Elaine might not be married to Rem right now. That wouldn't ease the pain of loss, though.

"I'm sorry," she finally whispered.

Rem seemed to shake himself. "I'm sorry your welcome hasn't been better. It's my fault for getting married the way we did and not telling anyone. Goes back to leaving and the fight with my dad and my brother's issues…" He sighed. "They're upset with me, and they're taking it out on you. I hate that, but with my dad the way he is, I don't want to leave because of it." He caught her chin with his hand. "Thank you."

For him. She was here for him, and she'd handle anything his family gave her if it helped make his last days with his dad easier or better, heal the past, and make the future bearable.

"What was it that he wanted to say?"

"Just that he was giving me the ranch. He's already changed the will. He did it last week. But he wants to put my name on the deed and make it official before he dies." Rem's jaw flexed—talking about his dad's death couldn't be easy—but his voice remained steady.

"That must be why Max is so upset."

"I'm sure." His hands rested on her hips. "Do you mind if we stop thinking about this for tonight?" His lips trailed over her temple. "I don't know about you, but that kiss you gave me earlier felt like I wanted more." He lightly bit the edge of her jaw.

Her body trembled, and she tried to focus. "I think you kissed me."

"Is that how it was?"

Her eyes were half-closed, but she could see his cocky grin. She nodded, shivering as his lips touched the corner of hers.

"Kiss me, Elaine. I'm not going to think about ranches, brothers, or death when your lips are on mine. I can't even remember my name when you kiss me."

She'd thought she was the only one with that problem. His words made her bolder, and she threaded her fingers through his hair, pulling his head down to hers. Their lips met, and the room and the rest of their problems faded away, leaving them the only two in the universe as it spun around them.

He pressed her to him, and her feet left the floor as he straightened. Their lips clung, and she barely noticed when he laid her down on the bed. His body pushed into hers as he lay half on her.

She wasn't sure how many times his phone had buzzed before she noticed it at the same time he did.

His head lifted, and he looked at her like he wasn't quite sure how they'd gotten in the position they were in. Then he grinned, his hand stroking her hair that was splayed out over his dark comforter.

"You look good in my bed." His drawl was deep and thick, and his words sent heat down her spine.

He sighed and kissed her quickly once more before he stood, holding his hand out for her and pulling her up. "I'm guessing that was my mother texting that it is time for us to show our faces at her dinner, and we haven't even showered yet."

Elaine squeezed him with her arm, laying her head on his chest, before letting go and moving away. "I'll shower quickly while you answer her."

~~~

Typical of his mother, "a few friends" had turned into twenty people. Elaine held out well, though. He supposed spending two years basically alone, running a ranch by herself while taking care of four young children, had given her the grit to at least make it through his mother's barbeque.

He knew everyone, and unlike in North Dakota, everyone here knew what he was and what he'd accomplished as a professional bull rider. They respected that and him. He hadn't realized how much he enjoyed just getting some credit for what he'd accomplished rather than being looked on with suspicion for being an outsider who may or may not have married Elaine for her ranch.

But his heart wasn't in the socializing. His dad and his declining health were forefront in his mind. It was hard to laugh and pretend everything was okay.

He caught himself longing to be back in his room with Elaine's arms around him and her body pressed to his. Her soft words in his ear and her quiet strength giving him balance and courage.

He held his drink in his hand and watched her smiling and talking to a young mother who lived on the next ranch over.

It scared him a little, to be honest. That he drew from her, almost depended on her, like she wasn't a separate person but was a part of himself. A part he needed.

He hadn't wanted to need anyone. Definitely hadn't wanted to depend on anyone.

He thought he remembered the preacher saying "two became one" or something along those lines, and he didn't have trouble believing it. Elaine had become necessary to him, making his old fears come true. But she wasn't like his ex-fiancée.

He'd not really thought of Olivia in a long time. Not until today when he'd seen his brother and the mess he was.

That had been him minus the booze after Olivia was done with him.

He'd thought that was the way women were, but after spending the last few months with Elaine, he thought, was pretty sure, she was different, that he could trust her not to be looking for the next best thing and chasing after it. That she was loyal and would stand beside him no matter what.

Someone came up to him and asked him a question. He turned away from watching his wife, but not before he thought to himself that he wanted to ask her how she felt about having more children.

Chapter 19

Rem ended up deep in discussion about bulls and semen, bull riders and the future of bull riding as a sport and whether bull riding in general had passed its heyday. He hadn't realized how late it was until he looked around and everyone except the people in his group were gone.

He looked again and saw that Elaine was helping the hired help clean up. She carried a big stack of plates and cups through the back door, following a woman with black pants and a white shirt.

Knowing Elaine had to be tired, he'd not planned to stay so long. Plus, he'd been looking forward to sharing a bed with her tonight.

It was that thought that made him stand abruptly. "I didn't realize it was so late. You guys didn't have to stay on my account."

"It's always great to see you, Rem."

The men took his cue and moved slowly to their feet. They couldn't leave fast enough for Rem. But when he was finally seeing the last straggler to their car, his mother texted him.

Your dad is awake and asking about you. Would you sit with him through the night?

He looked up just as Elaine came back out the door. She wore a knee-length jean skirt with flip-flops and a plain pink top. Her only jewelry were the rings that he'd given her. He hadn't realized until just now, but she was probably underdressed for the party. He wondered if she noticed or cared. She probably had. Which made him wonder if he'd hear about it later. Somehow he doubted it. In all the time he'd been with Elaine, she'd never bought a thing for herself. He hadn't realized.

It made him want to take her shopping. Except they needed every cent of their money to pull their ranch out of the unprofitable pit it was in and get it running in the black.

But if they moved here, like his dad wanted him to do, they'd be stepping into an already profitable operation. There would be a lot of hard work, yes. They wouldn't be pulling in enough money to be considered rich, but it would be enough for him to take his wife to buy a few clothes so his mother wouldn't be looking down her nose at her.

He texted his mom back then walked over to tell his wife where he was going.

~~~

Their flight home landed in Fargo before lunch. It was a sunny day, and thirty degrees would have felt warm if they hadn't just come from Texas.

Rem gripped the wheel tightly, knowing he had a few things he needed to tell Elaine. Things that probably weren't going to make her happy. Considering that his goals in life had shifted in that making Elaine happy had become the single, top goal, this wasn't a conversation he looked forward to.

He glanced across the seat. Elaine looked tired and preoccupied. Maybe the conversation could wait. Not indefinitely, but at least until tonight.

"How about when we get home, we take the kids and go see what they've done with the cabins? It's been a while since we've been to the lake." He needed to check them out anyway.

Elaine's eyes brightened. "I'd love that, and I'm sure they would, too."

"Wasn't that your mom that called last night? With everything that was going on with my dad, I forgot to ask if she was okay."

Elaine picked at her jeans and looked out the window. Her chest rose and fell deeply before she spoke softly. "She said Corrie had called her crying because James wanted to take the money that I had given him and buy his half of the ranch back. I guess they heard from someone that you were leaving me and he wanted to move back in with me." She gave a humorous laugh. "I was surprised he still had the money."

Her hand twisted the material of her jeans while she looked straight out the windshield.

Rem checked the speedometer then looked out at the flat North Dakota landscape. He didn't even have any wind to distract him today.

Finally he couldn't take it any longer. "And?"

Elaine turned her Texas-sky eyes at him and blinked. "What?"

"What did you tell your mother?"

"About what?"

A muscle in his jaw ticked, and his knuckles whitened on the steering wheel. "About James?"

"I didn't tell her anything. She wasn't really asking me to, I don't think." She lifted one shoulder. "I feel bad for Corrie. If we had room, I'd offer to let her come stay."

He gritted his teeth. "What about James? You said he wanted to buy his half of the ranch and come back?"

Her brows twisted together, and she tilted her head. "I don't care about James. He can take his money and light a bonfire with it."

"His money could pay off the ranch."

"I'd rather have you and no money than James and all the money in the world. I'm married. That means something to me." Her eyes softened. "I don't know how James could even think for one second that anyone could go to him after being with you. James is a nonissue."

He'd known it. Of course, he'd known it. But maybe after the couple of days in Texas, seeing his brother again, all the memories that were associated with that painful part of his past, he'd just needed to hear it. His heart rate eased, and he gave her a grin. "Thanks."

"It's just the truth."

"I have something I need to talk to you about."

"I suspect I know what it is." She was back to wrapping her fingers up in her pant leg. He hated seeing her nervous with him. He placed his hand down, palm up, on the seat between them.

She looked at it then him, smiling a little before she placed her hand in his.

"What do you think it is?" he asked, more because he wasn't sure how to start the conversation.

"Your dad is giving you the ranch, and you want to move to Texas."

His jaw dropped. "It's true that my dad wants to give me the ranch. And there will always be a part of Texas in my heart. I love the hill country, I can't deny it. But we're building something, you and me, in North Dakota, and I'm not just going to leave it for the latest shiny object that dangles in front of my eyes."

Her hand squeezed his, and she let a shaky breath out.

"I wanted to talk to Max, but he disappeared, and I needed to spend time with Dad; I might not get another chance." That thought caused a lump to stick in his throat, and he swallowed before he continued. "I told Dad if he didn't divide the ranch up evenly, I was going to do it the first chance I got." He huffed a laugh and gave her a sideways glance. "Of course, he threatened to leave the ranch to the government to make a park or something, but that was all hot air."

He looked back at the road, the miles of straight highway stretching out as far as he could see. The muddy islands of bare ground surrounded by a sea of melting white snow.

"Dad's going to buy Max a plane ticket and send him up here at some point. Hopefully Max can get himself straightened out and be able to run the ranch down there. If not, we'll hire someone to run it until Mom dies. He's provided money and other assets for her, by the way."

"You'd said before that your bull riding money paid for the ranch?"

"Yeah. But it doesn't matter. I'm not trying to make sure that I get every cent that's coming to me. Max is more important."

"Even after what he did to you?"

"Yes. And I think you understand."

They exchanged a look about their shared trial.

"So…if that's not what you wanted to talk about, what was it?"

He didn't know any other way than to jump in. "Sometime while we were on the plane, I got a call from the oil well company. You can listen to the message, but basically, he wants me to start as soon as I can. Tomorrow, if possible."

Elaine's eyes had gotten as big as saucers, then her head turned, but not before he thought he saw tears fill them.

Yeah. That's what he'd been afraid of. He didn't want to leave. Didn't even want to think about it. And while there was something nice about the fact that Elaine didn't want him to go, he knew one of her biggest hurts was that James hadn't loved her enough to stay. He didn't want this to become a shadow of that for her. But he didn't know what to do to stop it, because he had no choice—if they were going to save the ranch, he had to work the oil wells this summer.

~~~

By the time they'd gotten home, Elaine had pretty much resigned herself to the idea that Rem was leaving in the morning, probably early.

She'd handled four kids and a ranch before, she could do it again. And it wasn't like he was staying gone all summer; he'd have time off when he'd be home. Part of her whispered, *if* he came back.

But it was Rem. He was coming back.

She didn't know how long he'd stay, and if they were so desperate for guys that they'd call asking him to come the next day, he might not get the time off that he'd been promised. So she put on her happy face and determined that his last memories of her would not be ones where she was sad or pouting that he was leaving.

The kids came running out on the porch when they pulled up. They'd had a warm spell, plus the sun was getting stronger, and a lot of the snow was melting. Which meant that it was mud season. Elaine didn't care. She was just happy to see her children, and maybe she was a little emotional, too, since Rem was leaving.

They thanked Nell who left shortly after, driving away in her pickup.

Rem held Carson in one arm, and Elijah had a hold of his other hand. "How would you guys like to go on a picnic?" he asked, looking over their heads at Elaine.

"Yay!" they shouted. Even Gabe couldn't stop from jumping up and down in excitement. Banjo wagged his tail so hard his whole butt shook from side to side. The porch listed more than usual, and Elaine just hoped it could hold up to all the action.

"Let your mother and me get in and catch our breath. I'll run out and check everything in the barn, then we'll get packed and go to the lake."

Elaine gave Heaven a hug, then Heaven helped her carry the few bags of picnic supplies they'd brought.

Gabe and Elijah went out to help Rem, while Elaine packed the food with Heaven and Carson. They chatted about what had happened while she'd been gone, and she told them how big and beautiful Texas was. She didn't mention how nice and warm it was there, since there was no point in wanting what one couldn't have.

The rumble of a motor brought them all to the doorway. Make that two motors.

Rem came around the barn on a four-wheeler. Gabe followed him on a second one.

Elaine walked out onto the porch and stood with her hand on her heart. She knew Rem had been working all winter on fixing various pieces of equipment, but she hadn't realized those old ATVs could even be salvaged. That would make checking on the cows so much easier once they were let out to their spring pastures.

Rem parked in front of the porch with Gabe pulling up behind him. His eyes were hidden behind his dark shades, but his old cocky grin was back. Elaine had to smile back, despite the heaviness in her heart.

He shut it off and swung a leg over.

"You're not riding with us?" Elaine asked. She figured if they both hauled two kids, they could all fit on the four-wheelers.

"Nope. It's about time those hayburners in our barn get out and earn some of their keep."

"He's going to get the horses out!" Heaven squealed and jumped off the porch, taking two steps across the walk before launching herself into Rem's arms. "You are, aren't you?" she yelled, grabbing his face between her little girl hands and peering into his eyes.

"I'm not getting 'em out."

Her head tilted, and her smile slipped.

"Figuring you can do it."

Elaine might never be a horsewoman, but her kids had loved riding.

Carson ran in circles around the porch, stopping occasionally to grab Banjo and jump up and down. He might not understand exactly what they were doing, but he was excited about it, nonetheless.

Rem waited until some of the commotion had died down. "I assumed that you and I would ride these with Elijah and Carson. I'm only getting two horses out."

"That's perfect." Elaine's heart swelled with love and happiness as she watched Rem bantering with her children and the kids buzzing with excitement. How was it possible that ten dollars' worth of food, two twenty-year-old machines, and a couple of worn-out horses could make her whole family so happy?

It wasn't hard, but it took more energy than she had before Rem came. He'd made children and family something that was fun for her again rather than a bunch of chores she had to get through.

And tomorrow, he'd be gone.

She tried not to think about it. She didn't want to spoil today by borrowing tomorrow's worries. But what was she going to do? How was she going to survive without Rem who had become an integral part not just of her life but of herself?

She watched him saunter off, Heaven's hand in his, Gabe imitating everything about him from trying to match his long strides to the swinging arms and arrogant set of his shoulders and head. They were full of themselves and unafraid, but tender and compassionate, too.

Her eyes followed the slim hips, the broad shoulders, the jaunty set of his cowboy hat, and heat curled in her stomach. A little shot of nervousness twirled with it at the thought of tonight and what she might do.

Tell Rem she loved him, for one. Could she say the words out loud and not be completely embarrassed if he didn't return them?

Maybe she could do it in the dark.

Yes. She would wait until the children were in bed. She would say the words, then she would repeat the offer that she'd made before. Only this time, she would beg until he said yes.

Chapter 20

Rem lay on his side on the blanket that Elaine had packed with his head propped in his hand. Their kids, worn out from running around for the last three hours, sat or lay scattered around on the blanket. Even Banjo seemed all played out and lay stretched out on his side next to Carson.

Elaine sat, leaning against Rem's stomach, reading aloud a book she'd brought along. At first, he'd not been real interested in listening to the story, but he'd listen to Elaine's honey-smooth voice read about the social life of rocks and enjoy it immensely. But he'd been drawn into the story and now listened as raptly as the children.

Well, maybe almost. He had his hand on Elaine's waist and could feel her move every time she took a breath. It was distracting to say the least.

He'd played with the kids. One of them had found about six old kites in a box in the barn, and they'd had three in the air at one point despite Banjo thinking he needed to chase the kites, kids, and tails while they were trying to get them in the air.

No one in the family could be considered an expert kite flyer. They'd lost one in the lake when a strong wind took it down. Carson had let go of another one. Rem and Banjo had both chased that one. In vain.

One of the old strings was dry-rotted and broke. That kite was gone as well. It'd probably land in some Ohioan's yard tomorrow afternoon or so. Too bad they hadn't thought to put a message on it.

But they'd had success with the other three. Short-term success, since once he'd gotten them in the air, and had three of the kids holding them, he'd been more interested in trying to kiss Elaine than watching the kites. What else could go wrong, right? There weren't any electric wires for miles.

Somehow, before he'd gotten his lips past the sensitive spot just below her ear, the kids had gotten all the kite strings tangled up so badly that he'd not been able to untangle them and had to cut the lines. They looked kind of pretty sailing away.

"Guess we need about a mile between them next time we put kites in the air." He'd grinned at Elaine, who'd smiled back at him. The same smile she'd worn all afternoon. It wasn't the smile that lit up her face and made her look so beautiful he could hardly stand to look at her. Rather, it was the one that said she was going to fake it 'til she made it.

He thought maybe she was upset about him leaving. Whether that was because she was going to miss him or because she was angry that he was going at all, he wasn't sure. They'd never really agreed on it, and she'd been against it.

If they were going to keep the ranch, though, it wasn't something they had a choice about.

They'd taken a hike around the lake. He'd taught Gabe and Heaven how to skip rocks. And when they'd asked him if the Loch Ness monster lived in their lake, he'd shrugged and said some night they'd have to come up and do a stakeout, just to see if they could catch a glimpse of her.

Which, of course, made Elaine huff and ask how he knew for sure the Loch Ness monster was a female.

He'd winked and said he was sure of it because she made a man do crazy things just to get a glimpse of her.

Elaine's ears had turned red, but he hadn't felt bad for teasing her. He should do it more often. Money was scarce, and there was an unending amount of work that needed to be done, but they'd be wasting their lives if they didn't walk through the fire with a smile.

Plus, her smile helped to give him the strength to do what needed to be done. As much as he didn't want to, he'd feed the stock in the morning then get in his pickup and drive northwest to the oil fields.

But now, with her fluid voice caressing his ear like velvet and her lithe body warm and alive under his hand, he didn't want to think about the morning and how hard it was going to be to leave and especially about how Elaine might be comparing him to James in some way and wondering if he was coming back.

He didn't think she would. But it had to do something to her to see him go. She'd been expecting her life to get a little easier once she got married, but she was back to where she started, alone with four children and a ranch to run by herself. Only now, she might have guests in these cabins to cook for, too. Plus the cleaning to do.

His hand tightened around her, and he forced it to relax when her voice stumbled. He hated the thought of her working even harder. Hated thinking about her being here with strangers he didn't know. It wasn't that he didn't think she could handle herself. She might be slight and have the ethereal looks of an angel, but he knew she was stronger than she looked and fierce if necessary.

But it was his job to take care of her. Instead, he was leaving her. He had to quit thinking about it, or he'd end up staying home and selling the ranch.

He could do that…and move them all to Texas.

Elaine would go, and he was pretty sure she'd go without a complaint. But her heart would be broken. He wasn't doing that to her.

Plus, even though a part of his soul would always live in the Texas Hill Country, and he hoped that his family could spend a few weeks or more there every year, he'd fallen in love with Elaine's state. It was a state that would never lack for challenges—the cold, the wind, the snow. And that was just winter. It was a lot like Texas, too, with the big sky and the independent, self-sufficient people.

Maybe they'd always consider him an outsider, but he felt like he fit in and belonged here.

The sun had sunk below the mountains, and a shiver passed through Elaine. He shifted, moving until he sat with her between his legs, her back pressed to his front, thinking to keep her warm that way.

When the chapter was over, she closed the book and slowly set it down on the blanket.

The kids groaned.

"Just one more chapter, Mom?" Gabe asked.

"Mr. Rem and I have something we need to tell you," she said, low and soft, like she didn't really want to talk at all.

"Is he going to be our new dad?" Heaven asked.

Because of their position together, he felt a small shock go through Elaine. Or maybe it was him. He hadn't even been thinking of that. But it warmed his heart that Heaven would suggest it. What would Elaine say? Especially since he was leaving. Would she hold that against him?

"I think, if you want to call him 'dad,' you can." Elaine twisted, looking at him.

"Sure," he said, knowing his turned-up lips showed how ridiculously pleased he was.

Heaven smiled shyly. He leaned over and ruffled her hair. "Kiddo."

She crawled over and imitated his gesture on his head. "Daddo."

Which seemed to unleash the other kids, and it became a bit of a free-for-all for a while as the kids climbed on him, ruffling his hair and calling him "Daddo."

When things finally settled back down, Elaine cleared her throat. "That's not exactly what we needed to talk to you about."

Little, happy faces turned toward her again.

"In order to make sure that we have enough money to pay our bills, we are going to be renting these cabins out."

Again, he was ridiculously pleased that she'd decided to share a little more with the kids as he'd suggested. He was sure it would be better for them in the long run if they knew what was really happening, especially if they were given the option to help.

"We'll all need to pitch in to help clean the cabins, and we're going to cook some for the guests who stay here as well."

"Tomorrow, Mommy?" Elijah asked.

Elaine's breath huffed out in a little chuckle. "No. But soon."

The kids looked at her with big eyes.

"We'll help you, Mom," Gabe said.

"Well, Gabe. I'm going to need you to help with the stock. The cows are going to start to freshen soon, and we'll need to keep an eye on them."

"Oh, yeah. I always help Rem, um, I mean, Dad."

"That's the next thing. Mr…uh, Dad has been offered a job working the oil fields. The money he can make there will keep the ranch going until we can get the cabins rented full-time. So, the better job we do on the cabins, maybe the sooner Dad can come home."

"Come home?" Heaven said, with a tilt of her head. "You mean he's leaving?"

"Yes. The way you work on the oil fields is to be there without leaving for a few weeks, then you get to come home for a whole week." Rem could tell she was trying to put happiness into her tone, like it was a good thing. That had to be hard considering she wasn't happy about it.

"When?" Gabe asked, his brows lowered down.

Rem's stomach tightened. Gabe was old enough to associate his leaving with James's leaving. He didn't want the boy to lump him in with Elaine's ex.

"I'm leaving early tomorrow morning, as soon as I'm done feeding. I'll be feeding early. So, probably before you get out of bed in the morning." Gabe was sitting at the edge of the blanket, and Rem met his eyes. "I wouldn't be leaving, except I need to make enough money so we can stay here, on the ranch, while we build the herd and get the cabins going and maybe a few other things moving."

Heaven's lips trembled, and she started to sob. Elijah joined in. Carson had no clue why everyone was suddenly crying, but he started bawling louder than everyone else.

Rem put a hand on Elaine's shoulder, just to let her know he was here for her, but he didn't have a clue of what to do now.

If he'd had his choice, he'd have left tomorrow morning without saying anything to the kids, but that would have been the coward's way. While it would have kept him from having to deal with this, Elaine would have been on her own to handle it.

He met Gabe's eyes over Heaven's head. Betrayal was clear on his face. His eyes narrowed, and he jumped to his feet, his hands fisted at his sides.

"You're leaving just like our last dad did!" he shouted.

"I'm coming back." There was no anger in his tone, but he said it firm enough that Gabe would have no doubt he meant it.

"That's what he said, too. He said he needed to leave to sort things out." If eyes could spit fire, Gabe's would be smoking.

"If I don't go, we're going to lose the ranch. If I do, we'll be able to stay."

Heaven had stopped crying long enough to hear what they were saying. "I don't want the ranch. I just want you and Mommy to stay together." She wailed then threw her arms around Rem's neck.

His heart cracked painfully, and he put his arms around her.

Elaine looked at him, biting her lip.

"Okay, guys, listen up." He waited until they'd all stopped crying. Heaven still leaned on him, and he had one arm around her, one around Elaine. "Your mom and I have talked about this, and we feel it's the best decision we can make." A few squawks of protest started, and he held up his hand. "Sometimes we need to make sacrifices—do things we don't want to—in order to get where we need to be."

He gave Gabe a square look. "I don't want to leave. I want to be here, and I want to be with you all. But in order for me to have that eventually, I need to leave now."

Gabe still had a mutinous look on his face, and his arms were crossed, but he didn't say anything.

"I'll need to talk to your mom, but I think we can give it until this fall or maybe until Christmas. If the cabins aren't working out, if things aren't going the way we want them to, if it's too much work for your mom, then I'll quit the oil wells, and we'll sell the ranch and do something where we can all be together all the time." He moved his hand down Elaine's arm, so thin and delicate under his hand, and he wondered anew if she could stand up to the work that was going to need to be done.

"Does that sound good to you?" He bent down, speaking against her cheek.

She nodded. "He's right. We all need to pitch in and maybe do some things we don't want to. But we won't do this forever. If it doesn't work out, we'll try something else."

"But he's not coming back."

"He is," Elaine said firmly. "This isn't the same as what happened with James. Rem is doing this to help *us*, not because he wants something better for himself."

His hand tightened on her arm. Her faith in him was humbling.

The kids weren't happy, but they were no longer crying.

Rem wished there had been a different ending to this day, but at the same time, he was happy they had a great day to look back on while he was gone.

~~~

Rem and Gabe fed while Elaine bathed the little kids. They were mostly recovered from being upset, especially after she showed them on the calendar how they could count the days until he came back. There were still a few sniffles as she walked out of their rooms, although Rem and Gabe must have talked some more while they were feeding because Gabe's attitude was completely different. Elaine was pretty sure Gabe was going to be a big help while Rem was gone.

Elaine walked slowly down the stairs, wondering how she should approach the subject that sat at the top of her mind.

She'd told him the last time that her offer stood, but he hadn't taken her up on it. Maybe that meant he didn't want to. Logically, she knew that's probably exactly what it meant. But her heart had been arguing fiercely that he wouldn't have touched her today, wouldn't have snuggled up to her on the blanket, wouldn't kiss her, if he didn't want her.

She thought she remembered that he'd said he wanted her. If not then, when?

She'd promised herself she was going to approach him tonight, thinking she'd say something to him when they normally talked after she put the kids to bed.

It might be easier to wait until he laid down on the couch, and she could just come out in the dark and...

She put her foot on the landing and turned, taking the last three steps down, her eyes going immediately to where Rem usually waited for her, leaning against the bathroom doorway.

He was there.

But he'd left his shirt off and only had a towel wrapped around his waist.

Her heartbeat shot up like a rocket, and her breath came hard and fast.

Her eyes swept over the broad shoulders and the smooth, dark skin of his chest, lower to the well-defined abs, then back up until they slammed back into his, dark and hot.

She shivered. But she wasn't wondering anymore if he wanted her.

He pushed off the doorjamb, and she met him halfway across the kitchen. They stopped in front of each other, not touching.

"A couple of months ago, you told me I could move into your bedroom." His voice sounded like he'd dragged it across the barn roof on a hot summer day.

"Yes, I did."

His fingers flexed at his sides. "I don't want to be there because of your pity or your sense of duty."

She shook her head. Those thoughts didn't even enter her head.

"I was hoping, eventually, that we might be able to give Heaven a little sister."

Her breath caught.

"But not tonight, because you don't need a pregnancy to deal with on top of everything else we've got going on in the next six months."

"I'm worried you won't come home, Rem. It's dangerous work. If there's a baby, girl or boy, there'd still be a part of you here." She put a hand on his chest.

He put his hand on top of hers, his expression fierce. "No. Not another child to raise on your own."

"Then just make sure you come back." She closed the distance between them, lifting her face and wrapping her arms around him.

He put his arms around her, pulling her tight. "I'm gonna assume you're not prepared for this. I've been thinking about us together. A lot. But it didn't occur to me until you were on your way down the stairs that I don't have any way of making sure I don't leave you with child. I can't do that, Elaine."

"It was just a couple of hours ago that we told the kids we might have to sacrifice now to be able to have what comes next. A year from now when we're holding our baby, it will be worth whatever sacrifice we have to make."

"It's too much for you to give."

"Have you forgotten? We could move to Texas. I'd rather give up the ranch than give up this night with you."

He searched her eyes. "You don't mean that."

"I do." Her hands ran over the smooth skin of his shoulders. "I absolutely do."

A shudder went through his body. "I love North Dakota, and I don't want to leave it, but I hate leaving you here by yourself. I'm definitely not doing it if you are carrying my child."

"Then don't."

Like he couldn't help himself, he kissed her forehead and her temple and nuzzled down her cheek. "Okay. I get to spend the night with you. But if there's a baby, I'm coming home and we're going to Texas."

"That's fine." She closed her eyes, feeling the scratch of his cheek, the smooth glide of his lips.

"You'll tell me?"

"I'll call you as soon as I know."

Their lips finally touched.

~~~

Rem lay beside Elaine, their legs tangled together. One arm rested in the curve of her waist as she lay snuggled beside him. The other cradled his head as he admired the glow of her hair in the moonbeam that tracked through the window.

Tonight had probably been a mistake. How was he supposed to leave her now? Now that he knew what he'd be missing.

It was two thirty. Elaine had only fallen asleep twenty minutes ago. He wouldn't wake her, as much as he might want to.

He needed to get up in thirty minutes anyway to feed.

He had to remind himself why he was leaving, that it was only for a short time, because there wasn't anything in the world he'd rather do than what he was doing right now.

A phone buzzed.

Not his. It was out in the living room with his clothes.

He hadn't been real careful when he'd thrown her jeans aside, and he thought the buzzing was coming from the bottom of the bed. No call in the middle of the night was ever good news, but it usually constituted an emergency.

Moving carefully, he reached down toward their feet, feeling around until his hand brushed her jeans and found her phone.

He turned it around. Just a number he didn't recognize. Probably a telemarketer. But what could they be selling that was so important they could call someone in the middle of the night and expect a sale?

It didn't make sense.

Elaine moved, but she probably wasn't going to be awake enough to answer.

He swiped. "Hello?"

The person seemed surprised to hear a man's voice because he stumbled around for a second before he said, "I'm looking for Elaine Anderson?"

"I'm her husband. What do you want?"

"Her husband?" Surprise laced the man's tone.

"Yeah." The word was clipped.

"This is Mr. Peregrine, Esquire. My secretary made a mistake a few months ago. Elaine Anderson was told that she was sent a letter by mistake. Well, the mistake was that there was no mistake."

Maybe because it was two thirty in the morning, but nothing the man on the phone had said had made any sense to him at all.

"I've been sick, and I'm just now going through my records, trying to get everything straightened up. I know this is not a normal time for a telephone call, but I felt this was important."

"Okay."

"Sir, may I speak to Elaine, please? I need to know what account she would like the money deposited into."

"What money?"

"The one billion dollars that she inherited when she married you."

~~~

"I thought you weren't going to be here this morning?" a sleepy Gabe said when Rem walked in the door while he was eating breakfast.

Elaine had turned from the stove at the sound of the door, and Rem looked over the table at her, holding her eyes as he closed it slowly. Everything that had passed between them last night seemed to hover in the air around them. The phone call seemed surreal, and maybe to some people it would be the most important and unbelievable thing that had happened, but not to her. It faded next to all that had transpired between Rem and her. Her body ached, a good, sweet ache, and she knew she hadn't imagined any of it.

If she doubted, the look in Rem's eyes as he stood by the door would have confirmed it all.

"If you don't want my boots walking across your floor, you'd better get over here and kiss me." His voice, not quite as low as it had been last night, sent curls of warmth tangling up her spine.

She didn't even set the spatula down. Heat filled her cheeks – she wasn't used to having everything she'd done the night before flash before her eyes prior to breakfast – but she couldn't think of anything else with Rem's dark eyes following her around the table.

The hotter her cheeks got, the more his eyes crinkled, but his arms opened and she walked into them and nothing had ever felt more right.

"I'm not finished outside," he murmured in her ear, "but I wanted to say something to you now, because it's true no matter what the bank account looks like today."

She held onto his waist, but pulled back to look into his eyes, her heart full.

His hands cupped her face, the roughness of his calluses skimming across her soft skin. His black eyes were dark and sincere. "I love you, Chica." His thumb skimmed across the ridge of her cheekbone. "Nothing that happens today, or any other day, is going to change that."

"I love you, too, Rem." Her voice came out with that extra husky note in it.

His eyes flashed. Then, the familiar, cocky grin lifted his lips. "I know." His grin widened as her blush deepened.

"Mom and Dad are being mushy." Gabe's voice sounded disgusted as Heaven came down the stairs.

"Well, Gabe. I'm not an expert on this stuff." Rem pulled her close again and she lay her head on his chest, while his hands rubbed over her back. "But your mother needs the mushy stuff. She'd probably like to know that you love her too." His hands stilled, and his arms tightened. "Actually, I kind of like the mushy stuff, myself. Hearing your mother tell me she loves me is better than bacon and eggs and all the sweet rolls in the world."

Elaine laughed against his chest. "I'm better than food?"

"Better than food, than bulls, than steers ready to butcher." He took her chin in his fingers and tilted her head, making sure her eyes met his like he wanted to make sure she could see everything on his face and in his heart, as the humor in his eyes dissipated and they became as serious as she'd ever seen him. "Better than money, even a billion dollars. Better than a ranch in North Dakota or Texas." His fingers left her chin and traced her jawline back until his hand curved around the softness of her neck. His voice lowered. "I just wanted to make sure you know that. I know this started with a ranch and money, but that's not what I care about or what I want now. Not…what I love." He swallowed. "Not like I love you. And our children."

Elaine bit her lip. He'd seen her cry once, but that was a completely different situation.

Before she could gather her voice to say anything, Gabe's voice came from the table. "Is that why you're not leaving? Because you love us?"

Rem's head lifted. "No, Bud. Sometimes a man's got to do things he doesn't want to do, to provide for and protect the people he loves. That's why I was leaving."

"But you're not anymore?" Gabe's voice held hope, but also confusion.

Rem fingered the hair at the base of her neck. "We got a phone call last night that might change our financial situation. Since that was the only reason I was leaving, I figured I'd stick around this morning and keep an eye on our bank account. If we get the money we're supposed to, you can bet the farm I'm not leaving your mother and you guys."

"When will you know?"

Rem's shoulders moved. "Sometime after nine, probably."

Two sets of eyes looked from their parents to the clock on the wall. They both slumped in their seats.

"Then we won't know until we get home from school."

Rem breathed out a little heavier, but didn't say anything. Elaine appreciated that he allowed her to make the decision, not that she would have fought him about it either way.

"I think today might be a good day to stay home."

She'd barely gotten the words out of her mouth when Gabe and Heaven yelled and shot up from the table. They ran over to where Rem and Elaine stood by the door, their arms going around them both. Rem's hands loosened from around her and moved to encompass their kids, too.

Later than night, as she lay in her husband's arms, Elaine snuggled deeper into his embrace before kissing his bare shoulder and speaking softly. "I wanted to tell you this morning before the money came, but I think you know it didn't matter to me anymore."

"What?" Rem's chest vibrated under her hand and his leg shifted between hers.

"I married you to save the ranch and get the money, but somewhere along the way, I lost that pushing desire to save the ranch no matter what, and all I really care about now is being a family with you and the kids."

"You'd move to Texas?" he asked, a small note of disbelief in his voice.

She didn't need to think about it. "Wherever you are. That's where I want to be."

"Guess we could sell the ranch and buy an island in the Caribbean."

Now he was teasing her. She moved her hand lightly over his chest. "You'd be bored."

"No way. I'd make a spear and become one of those native deep-sea fishermen."

"The ones that hold their breath for fifteen minutes at a time?"

"Yup."

"I can see you doing that, too. I think it'd be easier on my heart if we just stay here."

"More work."

"I'm not afraid of work."

"That's one of the first things I loved about you." His fingers trailed over her arm and she shuddered. He shifted. "I forgot to tell you, but Max called tonight while I was out at the barn. Dad's been in a coma all day."

Elaine moved her head, but couldn't see his expression in the dark. "You don't want to go down immediately?"

"We'll have to, soon. But I'm at peace with our relationship. I think Max is going to step up, too."

"That probably eases your mind."

"It does. There will be some things to deal with, and we'll need to spend a little time there, but now that the money – that neither of us cared about anymore – is in our accounts, I want to get moving forward on the renovations to the house and barn, building a herd and forging ahead with the cabins and a ton of other things to make this ranch prosperous again."

"I'm with you."

"That's what makes it all worthwhile."

Epilogue

Nell Eastler had never been in a fancy dress shop. All the pretty confections looked soft and inviting and her fingers twitched at her sides as she followed Elaine down the aisle.

"I think these will be your size," Elaine stopped in front of a group of dresses. Nell could see the big, black "3" above them.

"That's what size my jeans are."

"We'll try a few of these first."

Nell put one finger out and touched a sparkly pink sequin before she forced her dry mouth to open. "I can't." She'd never owned anything even half this nice. She'd feel like an imposter at a ball dressed in something this fine.

"Will you at least try it on?" Elaine asked.

Nell nodded and they picked out three dresses to take to the dressing room. Nell had been watching Elaine and Rem's children while they shopped. Now Rem had taken the kids down the street to get ice cream because Elaine insisted she wanted to buy Nell a dress for the ball in payment for all the times Nell had watched her children and not been paid.

Nell didn't tell her that she'd put an application in to be hired help during the big night at Sweet Water Ranch. A part of her really wanted to go to the ball. Not just because she'd never been to anything that fancy, but because a bigger part of her wanted to see the mysterious man who'd changed her tire again.

She stepped out of the dressing room and stepped in front of the mirror. She snorted. Her farmer's tan made the pink dress look hideous.

"Guess I shouldn't have been out planting peas and weeding the onions." And feeding the cattle, fixing fence and mowing hay. Disappointment speared through her, because the dress was full and sparkly and made her feel like a princess for the first time in her life. There weren't any dresses in the entire shop that would hide her arms which were three-quarters brown, one quarter white, thanks to her t-shirt sleeves. Then there was her brown neck.

"Yeah, can't change it now." Elaine sighed through her smile. "The pink looks amazing with your hair and eyes, though." She snapped her fingers. "Gloves! We need really long gloves."

The clerk helped them find a nice, long, white pair. Nell had to admit they took care of her arms problem, but her brown neck still clashed with the pink dress and the white of her upper arms.

Elaine crossed her arms and tapped her finger on her lips. "You know, I think if you had long hair, you could arrange it so that it hid the different colors of you neck."

At least Elaine was honest and wasn't trying to convince her that her farmer's tan looked good in the dress. If her whole body were that color, it wouldn't be bad, but because some of her skin was so white her veins showed blue and some of it was brown as a table top, she looked like a two-toned car from the nineties. The kind one only found in junk yards.

"What about a scarf or head-covering? This is for the ball at Sweet Water, right?" The store clerk stood beside Elaine, her bracelets clacking as she crossed her arms over her chest and peered up and down at Nell's dress. "It's a masked ball, so your scarf could be your mask, plus it could hide your red neck."

Elaine liked the idea, and before Nell could protest, they had her head and shoulders wrapped up in a foamy, pinkish white thing that felt soft as a day-old chick.

Elaine and she had already had the argument about the cost of everything, with Elaine insisting that since Nell had been willing to help out when Elaine didn't have any money, now that she did, Nell should be willing to take what Elaine wanted to give.

The cost of the gown and scarf was more than her grocery budget for the entire year.

"Now for shoes."

Nell took a quick breath. Elaine tilted her head. "What?"

"I have shoes."

"Something that will go with this?" Elaine asked skeptically.

Nell nodded. Completely serious, but not wanting, for some reason, to explain where the shoes had come from. She didn't understand it herself. The handsome man who had changed her tire hadn't seemed to even want to give them to her. And they didn't look like they'd fit her. But when she'd tried them on, they fit perfectly. Comfortably. Like they'd been custom made for her feet. She couldn't describe their color, but they would go perfectly with this dress.

The air around them stirred, like the shop door had opened and Elaine's head popped up. Her face melted into a lovestruck smile.

Nell didn't have to turn around to know that Rem had just walked in.

Another second later the kids called their mother's name and soon they were surrounded by little blond-haired bodies. Elaine gave them all side hugs, but she met Rem half-way across the store and hugged him full-on.

They smiled and whispered to each other for a few minutes with the kids stirring around them.

Nell stood in her finery and watched. She'd give up the dress and ball in a heartbeat to have a man who looked at her like Rem looked at Elaine. He didn't need to be a cowboy. His hands could be soft as velvet and he could drive a low-slung car rather than a work truck. As long as she could stay in North Dakota and putter around in a backyard garden with maybe a few animals on the side, she'd be way more than happy.

But anything like that was highly unlikely with the way things were going with her step-dad. He didn't pay her for the work she did on the ranch, and it was hard to leave when she didn't have a vehicle. Still, she would have found a way, except for her twin step-sisters, Beth and Brit. Beth would be fine. She was outgoing and angling to get out of North Dakota, and she would, soon. But Brit was a little…odd. Nell felt like Brit needed her.

So she'd stayed. She loved North Dakota, and she loved ranch life. She could stand her step-father, too. But she really wanted a husband and family of her own.

A man who looked at her like Rem looked at Elaine, and hopefully, one who would allow her to bring her step-sister along with her.

The image of the man who changed her tire flashed through her mind again. Somehow she didn't think he'd be staying in North Dakota.

"You guys ready to head out? We need to get home and feed the stock." Rem's deep drawl cut through the noise of the children.

"We also have our first guests coming to stay at the cabins tomorrow," Elaine reminded him with a pleased grin, which he returned.

He pulled her into his side.

"I think we've decided." Elaine gave Nell a questioning look.

Nell nodded. She might not even be able to go to the ball as an attendee anyway. Her step father was unpredictable. He favored the twins, as well. If there was any reason one of them couldn't go, it would be Nell staying home.

Normally she was fine with that. Social gatherings weren't her thing. She'd rather be out in her garden anyway. But for some reason, the image of that man tugged at her, and going to this ball, even as a server, was something she really, really wanted to do.

"Yes. If you're sure you want to pay this much, this dress is perfect." Nell nodded decisively. She might end up giving the dress to Beth to wear. But she was going to at least serve at the ball, just to see the man she'd dubbed Prince Charming, one more time.

~~~

Thanks so much for reading! To purchase the next book in the series, Cowboys Don't Believe in Fairy Tales, click HERE.

Made in the USA
Columbia, SC
08 May 2020